Crossroads

A HICKORY SPRINGS SAPPHIC ROMANCE

KARMEN LEE

For proof that love never truly leaves.
Like home, you can always find it again.

Content Notes

Here are a few notes for what you'll come across in this story. No spoilers intended, just so you know what you are getting into. Feel free to skip ahead if you don't want to read over these notes.

This read discusses the death of a parent, infidelity, and abusive relationships.

Chapter 1

KANDICE

K andice stared almost unblinkingly as miles of road swam by. The lack of light illuminating the roadways after leaving the few larger cities behind only added to her dark thoughts. Walking in on her soon-to-be ex-husband, Charles, balls deep in her now ex-best friend, Riley, three months ago was still damn near seared on the back of her eyelids. Even after his half-hearted efforts to make it work, including the worst attempt at marriage therapy, nothing had helped it fade away. If not for her hands gripping the steering wheel, she might have clawed at herself to feel something, anything other than the sickening pain of betrayal that had become a constant in the weeks and months since that unwanted discovery.

She tried to keep her rapid exhales quiet, but all the deep breathing techniques in the world couldn't stop her brain from continuing to relive what she considered to be the death knell of her marriage. Things between her and Charles had been far from perfect even at the beginning of their marriage. He hadn't always been the most communicative of partners, but she had never thought him capable of infidelity. He sure proved her ass wrong—and in the biggest possible way.

Kandice hadn't been able to keep from confronting them that first time. Riley's apologies had come in waves every few days until they petered out into silence. She had thought that Riley's absence and the therapy sessions meant things were on an upward swing. It wasn't until she had been sent some damning pictures of Charles and Riley continuing to meet that she realized it was all pointless and her marriage was done. Charles' nonchalant attitude, unapologetic for the pain he caused, finally drove her from the house she had spent years pouring herself into.

She had hesitated for a couple days before calling her mother and letting her know what was happening before packing up their son, Caleb, for a one-way cross-country road trip. The call to her lawyer was the next move. She had retained him a couple weeks after the first betrayal though she had hoped to not need his services. When he called back, informing her that Charles also had retained a lawyer and was happy to move forward with divorce, that was all Kandice needed to know. She had found herself not totally surprised by that until he also told her that Charles had not wanted custody of their son Caleb and was going everything short of signing away his rights. As upsetting as it was, she felt a small sense of relief. Kandice had been a stay-at-home mom since Caleb was born, and she wouldn't have had the money needed to fight Charles in a custody dispute. To hopefully keep him from changing his mind, she had left the bulk of her items behind, only packing what she knew she and Caleb would need.

Most of her elegant gowns and dresses, the jewelry she had received and the electronics she once used were still at the house, probably already in use by the snake she had unwittingly invited into her and her son's lives. Still, she felt she had gotten the better end of things. Caleb was far more valuable than a television or any of the other material items she would never see again. A clean break was probably the best thing that could have happened.

Her cell ringing broke her from her dark thoughts, but she didn't bother to glance at the screen before sending the caller to voicemail. She'd only been answering calls from one of two numbers since she got on the road and that wasn't one of them. It was probably Charles' lawyer. He'd tried to get her to sign some ridiculous document a week ago to keep her from the millions in their joint bank account. Her lawyer had thankfully been there to keep her from telling them all where to stick it. There was really no need for it. Kandice had already transferred what her lawyer considered a fair amount to her own individual account before she let Charles know she was leaving. If the man had already frozen the joint debit or credit cards, she had no idea. She didn't have any desire to use them anyway.

No.

That wasn't true.

She really wanted to go on an elaborate shopping spree and donate all of the items to the family members and friends she had lost contact with over the years thanks to being married to such a selfish, uncaring man. Hindsight being what it was, she could scarcely believe how she had let herself be convinced to cut off contact with the people who once supported her. Being alone with no one else to lean on except a snake of a friend certainly hadn't been a healthy situation. She could see that now. It was startling to realize how much of herself she had lost during her marriage.

"Mom?"

"Yes baby?" She breathed out a sigh. The silence on the open road had been so heavy; Kandice had almost forgotten she wasn't alone in her misery.

"Are we almost at Grandma's?"

Kandice glanced in her rear-view mirror at the curly-haired boy in the backseat. Caleb had been sleeping peacefully since the last rest stop. His excitement at taking an abrupt vacation from life had been tempered by boredom and restlessness after the first day had come and gone with no conclusion to their journey. His presence was the only thing that kept Kandice from breaking down in a heap against the steering wheel of her car or freaking out about what to do next. It had been a long time since she had to plan anything on her own without someone else's input and after the first stop on this cross-country journey, she had found it wasn't as easy as she thought it would be.

When looking at him, Kandice could almost say that the past ten years of her life weren't a complete mistake. He was definitely *not* a mistake by any means, no matter what his asshole of a father had said in the heat of one of his narcissistic rants.

"Almost," she said with cheer she didn't feel. "We only have about another hour or so and then we'll be there. Do you need to stop and use the bathroom?" It was already dark, the trees looking gnarled and claw-like in the faint moon light. She didn't really want to stop at some random gas station in the middle of nowhere Georgia. It had been so long since she'd made the drive at night that she wasn't even sure where would be a good place to stop.

"No. I'm good," he answered with a yawn before turning to look out at the darkness. Kandice couldn't even think of what to say. She was too busy trying to peer through the tears that threatened to fall as she navigated her way on the back country road.

Never had she imagined she would be coming back home again permanently.

Home. They had visited a few times over the years, but as Charles's controlling grip had tightened, they came back less and less. It hadn't helped that he had gone on camera and talked shit about their shared hometown. Kandice was sure people in town had been less than thrilled to have a harsh spotlight put over them. It had been almost two years since the last time she'd stepped foot in the small town of Hickory Springs, Georgia and even then, they had gotten a less than warm welcome from most. No one had been outright hostile, but Kandice had felt a distinct difference. Coming back permanently was going to be a massive change from being on the West Coast. San Diego and Hickory Springs couldn't be any more different.

"You think grandma still has those goofy chickens?" Caleb

suddenly asked with more excitement than he had had moments ago. His exuberance at something so small made Kandice think back to her own childhood when the little things like helping her mother gather eggs from temperamental hens was an event to look forward to. That was before life had gotten far more complicated and a lot less about the little joys to be had. Still, she couldn't help but smile at the thought of Caleb enjoying some of the same activities she had at his age. Going home meant stability and help while she got herself together and figured out what would come next for them.

When she first discovered Charles was unfaithful, she had toyed with moving Caleb and herself back home, but she had been operating under a haze of rage, betrayal, and panic. Now that she was a bit calmer, she still felt guilty about uprooting his life, but she could see that it was probably for the best. San Diego was expensive, and all of her friends were really Charles' friends. The fact that not one of them had reached out to her was evidence enough that if they had stayed, she wouldn't have had any support.

Despite her own feelings about returning to her hometown, Kandice knew that moving back was the best choice for right now. "She does. I'm sure she would love for you to help her out with them, plus your grandma told me she just bought an ATV," she said with enough enthusiasm to fool herself for a moment. "Maybe if you're good and help her in the kitchen when she asks, she'll let you take the ATV out whenever you want."

"Really?!"

His high-pitched reply made her wince, but she couldn't help but feel fondness for his never-ending excitement. Ever since hitting double digits in age, not much excited him, so she resolved herself to enjoying it while it lasted. If that meant blowing out an eardrum, so be it.

"Of course. I'll even show you some hidden paths your grandfather showed me when I was a kid," Kandice replied before signaling with her blinker and pulling off the road when she saw the sign for her town. At this time of night, there was really no need to signal. The last car had passed by almost twenty minutes ago and now all she needed to look out for were deer and the occasional rabbit that might leap out in front of their vehicle.

The closer she got, the more anxious she became. She could only hope that people knew she didn't share Charles' feelings about the town they grew up in. She had taken out enough money to live off, but it wouldn't last forever. Jobs were already scarce. She had reached out to the school district ahead of time after seeing a position open up in her old elementary school, but if that didn't work out, she knew she was going to have to scour to find anything else that would be reasonable.

Kandice drove on for a few more minutes and when she saw that Caleb had fallen back to sleep, she figured that would be as good a time as any to listen to the messages she had on her phone.

"Hello Kandice, this is Roger Cavalli. I'm representing your husband in the handling of your unfortunate separation, and I have a few papers to send you for your signature. If you could call me back at 010-664-2331 with your new address, we could get the ball rolling and get everything settled as soon as possible with a minimum of fuss. Thank you."

Condescending asshole, Kandice thought fiercely. He had her lawyer's number, so why the hell was he calling her? Clearly, it was a move to upset her, and she was pissed that it worked. She shook her head and moved on to the next voicemail.

"Kandice, it's—"

She deleted that one immediately. How dare that bitch even think about calling her? Kandice gripped the steering wheel tighter and tried to keep her rage in check. Somehow, she wasn't completely surprised by her husband's behavior, but the fact that Riley had been the one to betray her with him was almost too painful to think about.

She had met Riley, her supposed best friend, freshman year of college. They both had been trying to get the perfect picture and bumped into one another. They had quickly become friends, and Kandice had been there to help Riley recover from the demise of her own marriage. A few times she had even sent Charles over to help around the house, an action she felt foolish for doing now. Not once had she even had an inkling that something was going on until it had been staring her in the face.

The next two messages were from Caleb's old school letting her know his documents had been sent over to his new school in Hickory Springs. The last message was from her mother, and she hesitated before listening to it.

"Kandice, the key is under the mat. Food is on the stove and should still be warm when you get in."

And wasn't that always like her mother; short and to the point. Kandice could almost appreciate it now in a way that she never had when growing up. She drove on, car gliding effortlessly around a turn, passing no one at this time of night. She sighed in relief when she saw the sign welcoming their arrival to the quaint little town of Hickory Springs that would be their home for the foreseeable future. The trees gave way to Main Street and Kandice slowed the car taking everything in. She was surprised to see that in the two years since she'd last visited, they had actually gained a big-name coffee house, a bookstore, and a few new fast-food chains. Perhaps she wouldn't die from boredom after all.

Kandice continued on past Main Street, driving around a new roundabout that decorated the city center before leaving it all behind. She almost missed the dirt turn onto the road that led to her mother's home and had to lean forward as she navigated the dusty road. Soon enough, she saw the large farmhouse complete with rocking chairs and a bench swing.

This is all for Caleb. She repeated the thought to herself as she tried to will away the heavy feeling that threatened to settle over her. Caleb deserved family and stability, especially with the mercurial status that would be the next few months of their lives. No doubt his father would fight her for everything *except* custody and

7

wasn't that just a kick in the ass to their son: the fact that his father cared more about keeping his money than keeping him.

Kandice reeled her thoughts back in when she saw her mother on the front porch. It was surprising to see her up so late at night, especially after her voicemail. Still, she could appreciate it instead of sneaking in under the cover of darkness like a thief in the night. This was the moment of truth. Turning around and going back the way she came was no longer an option. She pulled into the driveway parking beside the rusty truck that had been her mother's true love since childhood.

"I didn't think grandma would be awake this late," Caleb said softly, his voice still muffled with sleep.

"Me too," she replied. Being under the same roof with her mother was just adding a whole new set of problems given the push and pull nature of their relationship, but it had to be done for the time being. There were no available apartments to rent unless she wanted to be damn near an hour away. No, living with her mother was definitely the lesser of many evils.

She took a deep breath before turning off the car and opening her door. The smell of freshly cut grass and hay assaulted her, and she could feel a sense of panic rising in her throat. This was real. She was really back home and away from everything that had become familiar to her. Her marriage was really over. She viciously fought it down as she heard Caleb get out of the car.

He didn't wait for her to say anything before walking up and wrapping his grandmother in a tight hug. A small smile came unbidden to Kandice's face as she saw strong brown arms wrap around his back and haul him up in return. Regardless of how she felt, Kandice knew for certain that she had made the right choice for him, and she retrieved his backpack from the floor of the backseat with a defeated sigh.

"Hurry up with those bags, child, and come in the house. It's going to start getting cold before too long and this is no California weather."

Kandice gritted her teeth, the lilt of her voice already shifting back into a southern twang with no effort at all. "I know, mama. We don't have much, so I'll be inside in just a bit."

Kandice turned her back to her mother and focused on gathering what little they had before shutting the trunk. Not even back in this godforsaken hellhole for an hour and already she was feeling like the angry teenager she was when she left all those years ago.

Kandice looked out across the corn field and sighed heavily before beginning her heavy trek toward the house. Stepping inside, Kandice could see that the house had been renovated since the last time they had visited. There were still the same knickknacks over the mantle and the old dining room furniture was still there, but the living room furniture had been replaced, and the walls had been brightened up with a fresh coat of paint. She looked around feeling uncomfortable and a bit confused by it all; she didn't know what to think.

"Drop your things by the stairs and come get some food in you before it grows cold."

"Yes, ma'am," Kandice called out, setting the two bags she had down along with Caleb's backpack and her purse. Walking past the staircase and into the kitchen was a bit of a mind warp. The kitchen had been completely updated with stainless steel appliances and a large window above the sink that gave an excellent view of the backyard and the barn beyond.

The counter now had a bar area where Caleb was sitting, his long legs kicking happily as he bit into what had to be a homemade biscuit. He was chatting with her mother, not bothering to swallow before talking and his audience gazed at him with fondness clear in her eyes. If Kandice were being honest with herself, she had noticed a change in him the last few months. Caleb had grown increasingly quiet and withdrawn at home, preferring to play video games alone in his room. She hadn't wanted to make a big deal about it, so she never said anything; a fact that she was starting to regret now.

The last time Kandice had seen her mother, Margie, she had been a bit haggard from taking care of Kandice's father as he slowly succumbed to Alzheimer's. It had been almost a relief when he passed, though she had been worried that her mother would soon follow despite being much younger than him. It seemed that the time since had been transformative for her because her once dry-looking hair now shone healthily, with the gray hairs blending handsomely amongst her normal ebony. Her skin had a healthy glow, and it was soft enough that she looked younger than her 52 years. Her large dark brown eyes had a twinkle in them as she conversed with her grandson and the shape of her nose made it easy to see that the two of them were related.

Thankfully Caleb took mostly after Kandice with looks. She didn't know how she would feel if he looked like a copy of his father. They both had thick curly hair, though Caleb's was browner than Kandice's own ebony locks. Where Kandice's skin was a warm beige, his was only lightly tanned and dotted with freckles. His eye color was closer to his grandmother's dark brown, while Kandice's was a greenish hazel like her father's.

"Did you hear me, Kandice?"

"What?" Kandice's focus shifted back to the two other people in the room, and she realized she had been standing at the doorway staring while Margie had been repeating her name.

"I said sit down and eat. You're making me nervous with your hovering." Margie eyed her daughter as if unsure. "Is someone following you? Are you in some kind of trouble that I need to know about?"

"No mom, nothing like that!" Kandice was quick to reassure her. She had explained to Margie about the impending divorce, but she had declined to go into the specific details about why.

Kandice moved away from the doorway and further into the kitchen. Truthfully, she was feeling a bit like a trapped animal. She could only hope that Margie would let things be before she started in with questions. She had explained things, but only on the surface. Kandice hadn't told her mom about *everything*. When she was in front of the breakfast bar, Kandice opted to lean across it, balancing on her elbows. Margie was still looking at her as if she were expecting more elaboration on the subject, but Kandice had no desire to say anything more about Charles or the reason for their impending divorce.

"Dad doesn't care where we are," Caleb spoke up. He eyed the silent adults before shrugging and refocusing back on his plate. Kandice could feel her face heating with equal parts embarrassment and anger. Before she could say anything, Margie's hand came down on top of her own, perhaps to force a little calm into the situation.

Kandice had to look away. She had hoped to keep the truth of why they had uprooted their lives so abruptly from Caleb, but that was foolish of her. He wasn't a baby. He knew that people didn't just pack everything and move for no reason. The funny part was, he didn't seem to be too torn up about it. She wasn't sure if this was a blessing or a curse.

"Kiddo, you know that isn't true. I'm sure your dad must be missing you." Kandice looked at Margie for help, but she just gazed back with an unblinking stare. She sighed before continuing on. "Your dad and I just have some...issues to handle."

Caleb paused for a moment before speaking up again. "He has a new girlfriend, doesn't he?"

A vice squeezed around Kandice's chest at his nonchalant question. "What do you mean new girlfriend? How do you know about—"

"I saw him kissing Riley a while ago." When he saw she was staring, he quickly continued. "You don't have to hide it from me. It's fine."

Kandice didn't know what to say. Her heart was pounding so fast she was sure Margie and Caleb could hear it. Everything was suddenly too loud and yet too quiet. Her stomach lurched with the need to get away. "Just...finish eating with grandma, okay? I need to go outside and make sure the car is locked up."

She barely made it out of the house before she doubled over, body heaving as she took in large gasps of air to keep from screaming her rage into the night. All those months of secrecy–of trying to hold it all in and keep a smile on her face for Caleb–and yet she clearly had failed to keep him shielded from his father's negligence.

With shaking knees, she squatted down in the middle of the yard. She had tried so hard to shield Caleb from the reality of their current situation, but what was the use? Charles had gotten what he apparently wanted; a newer model to fuck at night and no responsibility for the fallout. It would be Kandice who had to deal with Caleb's questions about why his father didn't call in the coming months. Kandice's heaving breaths turned into sobs as she buried her face in her hands.

What the hell was she going to do now?

Chapter 2

REBEKAH

"Guess who is back in town."

Rebekah sighed. She knew exactly who her friend and coworker, Emma, was talking about. She also knew she didn't want to get into it. Not right now. She was having a tough enough day as it was with her now ex-girlfriend Susan deciding they were off again. Even beyond the mess that was that situation, lately it seemed like everything was determined to knock her on her ass.

"I thought you weren't a fan of town gossip," she said as she leaned back against her couch and stared ahead at the television. There wasn't a damn thing interesting to watch on a Saturday afternoon, but she was wallowing. "Plus, aren't you supposed to be helping me feel better after Susan decided to break my heart?"

Emma rolled her eyes before waving away her words. "Please. That was no big loss, and you are not heartbroken, so don't even try it. That girl wouldn't understand commitment if it bit her on the clit."

Rebekah winced at the description even if it were somewhat accurate. She and Susan had been doing this song and dance half-assed relationship for the better part of two years. If Rebekah were back in Los Angeles, she wouldn't have entertained it for as long as she had. But unlike back when she was in college, small town life, especially in the South, didn't lend itself to having many dating prospects when you were gay as the day was long.

"Plus, her reasoning for this latest breakup was pure shit," Emma continued. She leaned forward and grabbed a handful of pretzels before sitting back on the couch as well. "How do you go on vacation for three days and come back proclaiming your love for someone you just met. It's ridiculous."

"It's lesbians."

"Bullshit." Emma's vehemence made Rebekah chuckle. "She's playing games, and I don't like it. Fuck her and the girl she rode in on."

Rebekah sighed quietly. Emma wasn't wrong. Even with the uncertainty of her and Susan's relationship, this newest development should be the nail in the final coffin.

"But enough about her," Emma continued. "Back to what I wanted to talk about. Kandice."

That name nearly had Rebekah choking on air. She wasn't oblivious to the goings on in town. She had known Kandice was back with her son in tow the day after they'd shown up. Hell, she probably would have known that night if not for her already being in bed asleep with her phone on do not disturb mode.

"There's nothing to talk about." When Emma gave her a look that clearly conveyed how she thought that was also bullshit, Rebekah shook her head. "Seriously. I haven't spoken to Kandice in years. Not since the end of freshman year of college."

That wasn't exactly the whole truth, but Rebekah didn't want to get into it right now. She could only take so much before she wanted to scream.

Emma hummed. "Well, I know that's a crock of shit, but I'll be nice for now and let you live in the land of delusion about what it could mean that Kandice is back in town without a ring on her finger."

"Thank you for being such a supportive friend," Rebekah

joked sarcastically. She popped a pretzel in her mouth and chewed furiously. An hour later they ran out of pretzels. Thirty minutes after that, Rebekah found herself wandering around the grocery store while Emma railed against the lack of chip options available.

"When I tell you those jalapeno chips are God's gift to mouths, I am not exaggerating."

Rebekah chuckled and shook her head. If she had been paying better attention, she would have realized the two of them weren't alone in the aisle and probably made her way to the nearest exit.

"Rebekah?"

She froze in place at that voice. It should have been unfamiliar and yet she knew immediately who it was. Turning, her gaze fell on the solo figure in the aisle with them. Kandice had always been cute, but her twenties had clearly been her time to flourish. Sleek black hair was pulled back in a thick ponytail leaving the graceful line of her neck visible. Her brown skin was luminous under the harsh lights of the store and her lips were full and damn near pouty. Rebekah wasn't sure what she had been expecting. She knew eventually she would run into Kandice, but she thought she would have a little more time. Now that the time was here, she didn't know what to do.

Should she give her a hug? They were several years removed from the last time they had been in each other's presence. And back then, there had been a husband, and too many things left unsaid between them.

"Kandice...hi." It wasn't the most eloquent and Rebekah almost kicked herself at how hesitant the greeting was. "This hellhole dragged you back in, eh?" That was a little better but still not great. Beside her, Emma had paused in her diatribe and was looking between them with a crooked smile.

"You have no idea," Kandice chuckled before rushing forward and sweeping Rebekah into a tight hug. "It's so good to see you."

It is? Rebekah was surprised, but she hugged back without a thought. "You too."

15

The two of them had been the best of friends from middle school until they both left for university. Rebekah had always admired the quiet strength Kandice had in contrast to her own more extroverted personality that often got her in trouble. She stepped back to get a better look at the woman Kandice had become.

Her runner's build was still the same, but she was a few inches shorter than Rebekah. Her subtle curves were poured into a loose blouse and skinny jeans that looked to melt into her skin. "How long have you been back?" The question wasn't necessary. Rebekah knew exactly when Kandice had gotten to town, but she was trying to cover for being caught so off guard and ill-prepared for this little reunion.

"Just a day or so," Kandice replied with a smile that seemed mixed with a grimace. "I told mom not to make a big deal out of it. We didn't really come back for a happy reason."

"Mmm, I understand," Rebekah replied with a nod.

"What about you?" Kandice asked, clearly trying to change the subject. "Why are you still here? Last I heard, you still planned to move to Nashville and become the biggest music mogul in the southeast."

Rebekah shrugged to keep from wincing. "That was indeed the plan. I think the last time you were in town; I was out in L.A. for graduate school." The plan had gone completely off the rails when she had gotten the phone call from her mom telling her about the recent doctor visits and diagnosis. After that, dreams were hard to come by, replaced instead by hoping for a miracle that never came to pass.

"That sounds amazing! Where we were in San Diego seems so different from L.A. Did you meet any movie stars? Maybe date a few guys or girls in the business?" She followed that up with an exaggerated wink that almost coaxed a smile from Rebekah.

"Not even close. I had gotten a few contacts, but then mom got sick, and I moved back here to take care of her." Rebekah said that without any bitterness. She truly wasn't bitter about moving home to help her mom. And after everything, she was glad she had gotten the time with her. "By the time she passed away, it had been a few years, and I figured I might as well stay. There was an opening in the elementary school for a music teacher, so I started teaching and here I am four years later training the next generation of munchkins. Emma is a teacher there as well, and I think if I left, she would probably drag me back as is."

Emma nodded. "I would. You can't leave me alone with these kids."

Rebekah chuckled and shook her head. "Plus, I'm still in my mom's house and I don't think I could sell it, even with her gone."

"Wow. I'm sorry about your mom, Beks," Kandice said, the old nickname sliding from her lips like there wasn't years of empty time between them. She placed a hand on Rebekah's and for a moment, the warmth of it had Rebekah awash in memories long forgotten. "Mama told me she had passed. How are you holding up?"

Rebekah's hand turned over without her realizing until she was grasping at Kandice's. "It's been okay; tough, but I really like the kids I teach, and I still make music in my spare time so I can't complain." She looked up into light brown eyes. "And now that you're back, it helps to have another familiar face in town to reconnect with."

Who the hell was she and what were these words coming from her lips? She was horrified that her mouth was apparently running the show now without input from her brain. Kandice didn't seem to sense the inner turmoil based on her open smile. Rebekah squeezed her hand briefly before reluctantly letting it go.

"I am definitely back for the time being. My son, Caleb, will actually be enrolling in the elementary school starting next week. He's in fifth grade, so not sure if you'll have him in class or not."

"Probably," Rebekah offered. "Most of the classes come through me for at least a few weeks. I'll keep a lookout for him."

Kandice's smile shifted, growing so fond it nearly made Rebekah ache. "You can't miss him. He's apparently a little mini-me just a few shades lighter."

"Ah. I heard you and the great footballer ended up tying the knot." That was an understatement. Charles was Hickory Springs royalty back when they were in high school and up until he dropped some unflattering comments about the town, you couldn't go a football season without hearing his name being mentioned. He'd been a couple years older than them, but when he got a scholarship to play football at a D1 school, the whole town was ecstatic. He and Kandice had been on and off then, but after graduation, news floated down the grapevine that they were on again for good.

At least, until now. Kandice's lips turned down in a frown and Rebekah almost regretted bringing Charles up at all.

"Yeah," Kandice replied, voice losing much of its cheer. "But we're getting divorced. I'm sure the news has already started spreading."

Rebekah wanted to deny it, but she also didn't want to lie to her. "Sort of," she answered carefully. She knew how rough it could be when you were part of the rumor mill. She'd had to suffer the pitying looks for months after her mom died. It was grating at times to answer the same questions repeatedly, so she wouldn't do that to Kandice.

"I heard of course, but I'd rather hear things from you rather than join the rumor mill."

"Oh." That one word was filled with so much relief that Rebekah felt her own breath release with it. "It just wasn't what either of us wanted anymore," Kandice finally replied.

"I see. Well, what do you plan on doing now?"

Kandice looked at her for a moment before her lips curled back up in a small smile. "Actually, I heard the school was looking to hire another English teacher, so I applied a couple weeks ago. I have an interview on Tuesday."

Rebekah forced a smile to her face though she was more than a little stunned. She knew exactly the position Kandice was talking about.

"That's great," Emma replied, speaking up. "I know there was some concern about replacing Mrs. Engelton. Not many teachers, new or old, really want to relocate to a town this small. When I moved here from Chicago, everyone thought I was weird when I said I preferred Hickory Springs."

Rebekah nodded. "True. When I moved back, the guy I replaced left after three months and never looked back. I'm pretty sure he moved to DC or somewhere similar."

Kandice shook her head, amusement clear on her face. "It does seem to take a special person to want to stay around here."

"Hey now! It's not *that* bad here."

"Rebekah, be serious."

Rebekah tried to keep up her serious expression, but gave up before she could finish her sentence. "I am being—okay no, you're totally right. It is boring as fuck around here sometimes. However, now that you're back, I think things will be much more interesting."

"Ain't that the truth," Emma said before reaching out a hand. "Also, let me formally introduce myself. I'm Emma. I teach fourth grade science and math."

Kandice looked between them before reaching out, shaking Emma's hand. "Sorry about that. I was just running my mouth."

"Totally fine," Emma replied. "You two were catching up and I didn't want to make it awkward by telling my whole story. I have a few things to grab and then I'll meet you at the checkout, Rebekah."

Rebekah nodded before turning back to Kandice. The genial mood seemed to be broken leaving a strange sort of tension bubbling between them. It made Rebekah long for the easy conversation they had been having.

"Well, I suppose I should go," Kandice said finally. "I promised mom I would grab the groceries and make dinner. You should come by sometime. It would be good to catch up more."

Rebekah nodded. "I would love to catch up more with you sometime. Maybe I'll see you at the school soon as a fellow teacher. Let me know if you want me to put in a good word for you."

Kandice's smile was wide and before Rebekah could move away, she found herself again wrapped in a tight hug. It took her a moment, but she lifted her arms returning the gesture. When Kandice pulled back, her lips were parted in a toothy smile that Rebekah was helpless to not return. She tried to ignore the warmth that spread through her, but as she moved away, she couldn't help but look back where Kandice still stood in the aisle.

Chapter 3

KANDICE

Three months since uncovering the lie of her marriage.

Two weeks since moving back home to Hickory Springs.

One week since getting a job at the elementary school. This was how Kandice was keeping track of the changes in her life. Somehow it had taken less than six months for her to go from being a happy housewife with a seemingly perfect life and marriage to a miserable guest in her mother's home. She had received another lump sum of money from what used to be her and Charle's joint account; though nowhere near how much he was truly worth, and nothing else. She hadn't even had to speak with him. On the contrary, the one time she did reach out all she had asked is how he had wanted to split up time between them for Caleb.

He hadn't.

He'd wanted to sign his rights away. When he'd found out that was unlikely, he'd instead given her full physical and legal custody with a sizable child support agreement with the understanding that he wanted no further contact until the divorce was done and they both needed to sign on the dotted line.

Kandice had merely sat, stupefied and unable to muster words; she had simply nodded and hung up the call. When she'd told her mother, Margie had simply shaken her head before walking away muttering about shit men under her breath. It was one of the few times Kandice had ever heard her mom curse, and she couldn't blame her. She wanted to do some cursing herself, but she held back in case Caleb walked in.

Since moving to town, Caleb hadn't asked to see his father, not even once. Kandice wasn't sure if that made her feel better or worse. What type of relationship had Caleb even had with his father? It made her wonder, had all the signs of their impending split been right in front of her even before walking into him balls deep in another woman? Regardless, it would eventually be all over and Kandice would be a single mother. She had never imagined her life ending up this way, a fact that had her lying in bed staring up at the ceiling even though she should be up and preparing to start her new job in a couple days.

"Get up, child, and stop being so damn dramatic!"

She sighed as her mother's voice called out through the bedroom door. For the past couple days, Kandice had taken to getting Caleb on the bus in the mornings and then staying put in bed, wallowing in her own self-pity. Sometimes she showered, oftentimes not. It wasn't like it mattered in her opinion. Other than the occasional walk into town or stopping by the grocery store, she hadn't really connected with anyone outside of Rebekah. It seemed that most of her classmates from high school had done the same as her and taken off at the first opportunity.

The smell of fresh biscuits made her groan as her belly let out an angry grumble reminding her that while she was content to do a whole lot of nothing, it did not feel the same.

"Fine. Traitor," she muttered, pushing herself up off the bed and throwing on a robe before leaving her room. The floorboards in the hallway hadn't been replaced in years, so they squeaked with each step she took. She descended the stairs slowly and when she walked into the kitchen, she saw her mother standing at the stove stirring something in a pot.

"About time you got up, child. You've been sleeping late every day this week. You're going to need to get in the habit of rising before the sun unless you plan on being late to work every day."

Kandice winced.

"Yeah, I know. Just tired still from our long drive out here, I guess. Moving is stressful." She sat at the bar and took one of the biscuits, still hot from the oven. She slathered on a good chunk of softened butter and strawberry preserves before taking a bite. She could readily admit that the food was definitely one of the perks of being back in her childhood home. Nobody could cook like her mother. Charles hadn't been a fan of the food they grew up with, preferring five-star meals that required multiple utensils and possibly a ball gown. She'd always been annoyed by that and had missed the comforting scents that always reminded her of warm kitchens and a full belly.

"Well of course you are, lying in bed like a bump on a log. If you'd get out and do something, you wouldn't be so depressed." Margie eyed her daughter with a knowing glint. It made Kandice want to hide away, but she forced herself to appear unaffected. She'd had plenty of practice hiding her feelings in her marriage and she called on that same strength to help her now.

"Sorry."

"Mmhmm." Margie let her gaze fall on the slowly dwindling plate of homemade biscuits. She seemed to be considering something, and Kandice waited patiently for her to say whatever was on her mind. When no other words were forthcoming, she looked up. Her mom was not normally a tactful woman, usually letting whatever she thought flow freely from her mouth, so her lengthy silence made Kandice uncomfortable.

"You need a hobby," Margie spat out.

"What?"

"Or a date."

Kandice sputtered trying to make sense of her mom's words. "What are you talking about? What do you mean I need a hobby or a date? Those are not even remotely similar."

"Yeah, well, you heard me," Margie replied, turning back to her pot. "You're not going to feel better sitting around here moping. That man has moved on; Caleb has moved on, and let me tell you. That kid knows exactly what's going on, so don't think you're getting anything past him."

Kandice blanked on that little bit of information. She had known that Caleb knew about the impending divorce, but she still hoped to keep some of the more painful details a secret.

"Where am I going to find a date, mama? It's hard enough to date in the city, never mind in a small town. Plus, I don't think I'm ready to even consider it. I haven't gone on dates in years and Caleb and I haven't talked about how he would feel if I got back out there."

"Well, you have to get back out there sometime."

Kandice shook her head. "The divorce isn't even finalized yet mama. I have too much on my plate for all that."

Margie snorted. "Well, find you a damn hobby then and get out of the house for once so I can clean the hell up."

"Oh," Kandice replied. It wasn't a bad idea. But... "Like what?"

"Chile, I don't know. This town has no shortage of things to do, so I doubt you'll have any problem. Now, I'm serious. Get the hell out of the house so I can clean!"

Kandice gave a little chuckle, the first genuine one she'd had in weeks. Margie looked a bit smug as she put a few more biscuits on the plate in front of her daughter. Her mom was right. She doubted Charles was sitting around moping about the end of their marriage, so why was she? She refused to let that man, and his wandering dick dictate the rest of her life. She resolved to get out of the house each day rather than sitting around worrying about things she could not control.

"You're right, mama. Maybe a hobby would do me some good," she conceded. Truthfully, she was getting tired of just lying around all day. They had gotten satellite TV, but even that got old after a few days.

"Of course, I am; been telling you that all your life." Margie said, putting her hands on her hips. "Now scoot!" She made shooing motions with her hands.

"Thanks, mama."

"Hmph," Margie replied, turning back to her pot. Kandice caught the small smile on her face and couldn't help but echo it with one of her own. She grabbed another biscuit from the plate before heading back upstairs. She had a couple days to get her act together and she refused to waste her time pouting about her past rather than settling into her future.

After a quick shower, she was feeling better than she had in weeks. The feeling didn't wane even as she drove into town and saw unfamiliar faces milling around. A large cup of coffee perked her spirits up even more and she decided to take a walk around the town center to see if there were any interesting shops to spend some time in.

Twenty minutes later she had found a bookstore complete with a small area in the front set up with comfortable couches that created a warm and welcoming atmosphere. Kandice combed through the stacks of edge-worn books and new titles before settling on one that promised steamy results in the bedroom.

Kandice scoffed.

"I seriously doubt this book would be enough to get my bedroom the least bit warm," she muttered, turning the book around to gaze at the back cover. The sight of an impossibly ripped, half-naked cowboy clutching the arms of a gorgeous heroine did nothing to entice her, but she reluctantly sat back and opened the book. At least she could live vicariously through someone else's written fantasy. If her mind replaced the male love interest with someone a little more curvaceous with dark brown skin and perfectly pouty lips, that was her own business.

THE SOUND of Kandice's shoes echoed down the empty hallway. She had spent the last couple days gathering supplies and preparing to step into a new classroom. The school district had been thrilled when she applied to replace Mrs. Engleton as the third grade Language Arts teacher at the elementary school. The older woman had been thrilled as well given that she was hanging on and delaying her retirement until the position was filled. Apparently, there hadn't been any other applicants, so Kandice's application was fast tracked in the system. Caleb hadn't exactly been thrilled to share a school with her, but he calmed when he realized she would be on a completely different hall than him. Kandice had promised him she wouldn't interfere and given that it was already nearing the end of October, he only had less than a year to deal with her presence before he would move on to middle school and leave Kandice behind.

She slowed her approach as she came upon the door to her classroom. The students wouldn't be in school for another day thanks to it being the tail end of their fall break, but she was still nervous. It had been years since she had had a job doing anything, and even longer since she had been responsible for handling her own classroom and group of students. Rebekah had been sweet enough to send her an email welcoming her to the team, but beyond that, they hadn't talked much since running into one another a week ago. Truthfully, Kandice wasn't quite sure what to say. Once upon a time, talking to Rebekah had been as easy as breathing before time and space seemed to get in the way. Kandice wondered if they would ever have that ease around one another again.

"Okay, just open the damn door," she muttered to herself,

hand resting on the handle. Her grip tightened and she turned it, wincing at the slight squeak that echoed down the hallway. Taking a deep breath, she pulled the door open and peered inside.

The classroom itself was tidy. Mrs. Engleton had done an excellent job of cleaning all her things out of the room. It had a distinct disinfectant smell that Kandice knew would eventually give her a headache, so she walked over to the windows and opened a few to let a breeze in. Her desk was on the side, directly across from the door which would give her an excellent view of all the students even when sitting down.

"Knock knock," Rebekah said, sticking her head around the door frame of the classroom. "How's it going? I came in a little early to check on you."

"That's so sweet of you. You didn't have to do that," Kandice replied with a smile. "I just got here, but I think things are going to be okay. Mrs. Engleton left me a nice packet of everything the class had done so far and some student profiles, so I was just going to review those before the morning meeting."

Rebekah nodded as she walked in. "Yeah, Mrs. E was great like that. I always went to her when I was looking for classroom management tips."

"I'm sure I will need all the help I can get. It's been years since I was in the classroom." Kandice tried to keep her voice upbeat, but she could hear the current of tension in her tone. This was a big deal for her. The settlement she would get from Charles was substantial, and the hefty child support would come in handy, but after resolving some joint debt she hadn't been aware of and buying some necessities, Kandice knew she would have to be much more careful with money that she had been before if she wanted to move out of her mom's house anytime soon. Apartments were few and far between in Hickory Springs as were properties that didn't need a ton of work. It was yet another reminder of her new reality.

"I'm trying to decide how to re-decorate the room so the students will enjoy it."

"As long as it is nothing like the room you had in high school then I'm sure you'll be fine," Rebekah joked.

"Hey!" Kandice exclaimed. "Boy band posters made excellent wallpaper."

"Uh-huh." Rebekah rolled her eyes with a smile. She walked across the room and leaned her hip against Kandice's desk. "So, heads up, they named the new principal a couple days ago."

"What?" Kandice stumbled slightly in surprise. The motion made her bang her knee against a shelving unit beside the desk and she hissed out in pain. She leaned down to squeeze her knee hoping that the pain wouldn't last too long. The old principal had been dearly loved having been at the school for nearly two decades. In fact, he'd been at school when he had the stroke that nearly ended his life. Thankfully, a few other teachers had still been around and able to get to him in time to call an ambulance, but it meant the end of his career. "They decided already? I thought they were still interviewing people."

Rebekah smiled and shrugged. "I thought so too. I came in this morning and heard people in the office talking about getting things ready for the new guy, and when I checked my email, the notice was there. He's apparently some sort of golden boy with the district. He only stays at a school for a few years, helps it get in shape or whatever that means, and then he moves on to the next one."

Kandice frowned. "Is our school in some sort of trouble?"

"If it is, I was never aware of it. Being a music teacher means I don't really have to concern myself with any major exams," Rebekah replied, tracing a pattern over the surface of the desk. "You should be fine though. They usually give grace to new teachers, especially if you start in the middle of the year."

"Oh." That bit of information calmed Kandice's nerves slightly, but she continued to wring her hands together. She was already nervous about going back to work, and this new bit of information only made things worse.

"Hey." Rebekah moved around the desk quickly to wrap Kandice in a tight hug, one hand resting on Kandice's lower back and the other tangling in her dark hair. She guided Kandice's face into her neck and hummed soothingly. It was something they had done as kids when Kandice's anxiety got the best of her. It had been so long since she felt a soothing touch that she almost jerked away in overstimulation. When Rebekah's scent of cloves and cedar brushed across her nose, Kandice found herself leaning gratefully into the touch. "It's going to be fine. You got this."

Kandice took a deep breath and held it for a moment letting all the tension bleed out of her. She could handle this. She knew she could. It was just jitters that would be gone as soon as she got over the cliff that was her first day.

"You're right. I know you are," she said softly.

Rebekah snorted. "Damn right I am. I should have recorded that just to have it on record for the next time you try to argue with me."

Kandice chuckled quietly as her hands settled on Rebekah's hips. "We haven't argued in years."

"There's a second first time for everything." Rebekah's words were teasing, but they still helped settle the frantic feeling in Kandice's chest. For the first time since she'd found out her life would change, she felt something akin to comfort. It was that realization that made her cling tighter, taking in as much comfort as she could before she knew she would have to pull away.

Chapter 4

REBEKAH

Rebekah hadn't intended to hug Kandice, but watching the way she twisted her fingers together, a nervous habit she'd had even when they were children, pulled at something inside her until Rebekah found herself enveloping Kandice in a tight embrace. They hadn't had a big conversation about why Kandice was back, but from the whispers she couldn't get away from, Rebekah was sure she knew what happened. What she didn't know was how Kandice was feeling about everything. Sadly, that conversation, if it ever came, would have to wait until they weren't at work.

With a sigh, Rebekah moved to pull away. Cool air rushed between them and when Kandice shivered, she wanted to reach out again. Instead, Rebekah clenched her fist. She was prepared for questions, but she wasn't prepared for the look in Kandice's eyes. They were half-closed as if she had just awoken from a dream. Her lips were parted as she sucked in a deep breath and Rebekah's gaze was locked on, unable to peel itself away.

"So..." she said trailing off when she realized she didn't know what to say. Kandice was looking for comfort and here she was stuck on the fact that she felt damn good in her arms. *Get it together.* "I'm sorry if I—"

"And this is our new third grade teacher."

A loud voice called out startling both women into jumping further away from one another. Rebekah did her best to try to look unruffled by the interruption, but her heart was racing at what had just happened. She was sure she wasn't imagining that for a moment, she and Kandice had connected in a way that felt distinctly more than platonic. There had been *something* there that had her recalling warm sticky air and exploratory touches under the quiet of a summer night. She smoothed her hands down her pants to give herself something to do until she could form words fit for a professional audience.

When she looked up, Kandice was standing there looking perfectly unruffled with a well-practiced smile on her face. It was so different from the nervous woman she had seemed to be when Rebekah entered. The abrupt switch was almost jarring. Who was this new woman before her? Footsteps had her turning to the doorway before she could make a mistake by asking.

An unfamiliar man walked in. He was tall, probably a little over six feet with broad shoulders that lead down to a trim waist. His skin was a warm tan and his eyes a piercing gray that took in the entirety of the classroom before settling on them. Mrs. Kaye, the school secretary, was still excitedly extolling the merits of the teachers at the school, completely oblivious to the tension that lingered in the room. After taking a breath, she turned and smiled.

"Oh, perfect. You're here too, Kandice. This is Mr. Robert," Mrs. Kaye called out excitedly. "He is our new principal. Mr. Robert, these are two of our teachers, Ms. Rebekah, head of our lovely music program, and Mrs. Kandice, our newest third grade teacher. She's a recent returnee and replacing one of our longest tenured teachers. It is so wonderful when people return home."

Rebekah immediately walked over to the man and extended her hand in greeting. It wouldn't do to seem standoffish, especially with him being the principal. She'd heard of his reputation for turning schools around, but no one did that without ruffling a few feathers. For a moment, she wondered if he were the type to come down hard on people from the start or if he preferred to warm up into it. When his lips split into a warm smile, she decided on the latter.

"Nice to meet you," she said, taking the lead.

"You as well," he rumbled out, shaking her hand with a small nod. He turned to Kandice who hadn't moved. "And you must be Mrs. Kandice."

"It's Ms. actually, but thank you sir."

Rebekah noticed how one of his eyebrows twitched slightly when corrected about that. Maybe correcting him on anything wasn't such a good idea. She noticed that Kandice might have come to the same conclusions judging by how her eyes widened and she once again tangled her own fingers together.

"Pardon me, Ms.," he replied smoothly, not seeming to take offence. "It's wonderful to meet another new recruit. I assume everyone has welcomed you home with open arms?"

"Yeah, I mean yes," Kandice answered before dropping her hands at her sides.

"I was just giving her the rundown about our upcoming meetings," Rebekah added in hoping to move things along. She didn't like the way Robert's eyes ran over Kandice's frame. He wasn't obvious about it, but Rebekah had been doing the same and she could recognize when someone was interested in what they saw. "The previous teacher left wonderful records and helpful notes."

Robert glanced at her and nodded. "That's good to hear." He turned back to Kandice. "So, what drew you back here to the school?" He crossed his arms and leaned into the doorframe deceptively casual.

"I missed the area," Kandice said. Rebekah knew that wasn't the real reason, but if it warmed her chest to think that part of Kandice might have missed the town and potentially, her, she would take that knowledge to the grave. "My mom and Mrs. E are friends and when she heard about her impending retirement, I figured maybe it was time to come back. It's been a while though, so I'm excited to see how the classroom has changed."

Robert nodded like all that was a perfect answer. "Well, I'm sure you will do fine. I'll make sure to keep an extra eye on you and don't hesitate to ask me for help if need be."

"Absolutely." She glanced at Rebekah and smiled. Rebekah couldn't help but smile back in return. "And I know Rebekah will help me if I run into trouble as well. Right?"

Not helping wasn't an option as far as Rebekah was concerned. "You know I will."

"Great," Robert said, drawing her attention again. Rebekah's eyes narrowed. His tone was friendly, but something about the way his eyes were trained on Kandice had Rebekah looking at him more closely. As if sensing her scrutiny, he coughed and took a step back. "Good to meet you both."

Kandice returned the sentiment as Rebekah nodded and watched him and Mrs. Kaye exit the room and head down the hallway.

"He seems nice."

"Yeah," Rebekah said though she wasn't sure she actually agreed. Something about the whole interaction wasn't sitting well with her, but she didn't know why. Her hackles were raised, but she tried to push away the feeling. "So hey, why don't we go do some quick shopping this afternoon for any items you might need to turn this place into your own little oasis of learning?"

"Sounds like an excellent idea," Kandice agreed. "We could probably grab an early dinner too. I think mom should be okay with watching Caleb for a little longer. She's been telling me to get out of the house for days."

Rebekah chuckled. "I can imagine being back was a little overwhelming at first. I know when I first got back, everyone was trying to be helpful, but it was a lot to deal with."

Kandice nodded enthusiastically, her head bobbing fast enough to almost make Rebekah nauseous. "Yes, exactly. I know everyone was trying to be nice and welcome me home, but I wasn't exactly ready for company. I'm still not, if I'm being honest about it." She swallowed before looking away. "It's not like I came back for happy reasons."

It was the closest Kandice had come to talking about things and as much as Rebekah wanted her to continue, they only had a few more minutes before they would be surrounded by the other teachers. "I know," Rebekah said carefully. "But, despite that, I for one am more than a little excited that you're back."

"Yeah?" Kandice asked. The vulnerability in her voice had Rebekah nearly tripping over herself to reassure her. She reached out and wrapped an arm around her shoulder.

"Absolutely." There was more Rebekah wanted to say. She wanted to tell Kandice that she'd missed her terribly when they first parted and how that feeling never really went away. She wanted to know all about the life Kandice had and whether she still remembered the jokes they'd shared. Before she could open her mouth, the intercom crackled to life calling everyone to the cafeteria for their staff meeting.

With a sigh, Rebekah followed Kandice from the classroom and tried not to let the questions left unsaid rob her of the happiness she had from her friend being back at all.

Chapter 5

KANDICE

"Jesus!"

Kandice blew out a breath as she flopped back in her chair. She was so unbelievably tired and wanted nothing more than a hot bath and her bed. She had survived her first week of teaching and she was almost shocked at how well things were going. She was expecting to crash and burn hard after having been out of the classroom for nearly a decade, but beyond navigating a few inattentive students nothing had been more than she could handle. It was an encouraging week and for the first time since she had packed her and Caleb into the car and set off down the highway, she was feeling sure of her decision.

A knock at the door had her head snapping up eager to discuss how things had gone. When she saw Principal Robert in the doorway, the kernel of disappointment surprised her. Truthfully, she was hoping it was Rebekah coming to see how her first week went.

"Oh, Principal Robert. Is everything alright?" She tried to cover her disappointment with a small smile.

"Remember, I told you all to just call me Robert if the students aren't around," he joked, tone chastising her slightly.

Shit, I forgot about that. "Right. Robert. My apologies. What can I do for you?"

"I just wanted to check on you and see how your week went." He made a gesture with his hands. "I know it can be a lot taking on your first classroom after an extended time away."

Kandice almost felt bad at being disappointed that it was him who showed up when clearly, he was just trying to be a good principal and a nice person.

"Oh, I think it went okay. All the students were well-behaved and there were no tears."

He smiled and nodded. "That's what we like to hear. Did you have any ques—"

"Hey Kandice. Ready to head to dinner?" Rebekah came around the corner, walking into the classroom and pulling to an abrupt stop when she almost ran into Robert's back. "Oh, Principal Robert. Nice to see you."

Robert's smile slipped slightly before he turned to Rebekah and nodded a greeting. "Ms. Rebekah. It's nice to see you as well. I trust the week went well for you."

"Absolutely," Rebekah confirmed with a quick nod. When her gaze slid past Robert and landed on Kandice, it was like being hit by lightning. Kandice sat up straighter, eyes locked on Rebekah as she took the other woman in.

She was wearing dark wash jeans and a school t-shirt with black cardigan on top. Her hair was pulled back into a low bun leaving her face free. Kandice's eyes slid over her cheeks wondering just how soft her skin would be if she cupped them with her palm. When they were younger, Rebekah had hated her slightly chubby cheeks, saying they made her look like a little kid. Secretly, Kandice had agreed but she still had loved cupping them, squeezing lightly to feel them give before plumping back up. She wondered how Rebekah would respond if she did it now.

"Are you ready or do you think you need some extra time?"

Rebekah asked, drawing Kandice's attention. "We don't have reservations or anything, so we can leave whenever."

Right. Dinner. Kandice stood up when she remembered that she and Rebekah had planned on grabbing dinner and a movie. Kandice had felt bad initially when she went to ask Margie about watching Caleb tonight while she went out for a bit. She hadn't expected Margie to practically tell her not to come home. *Maybe I have been bothering her.*

"Oh, you two already have plans?" Robert asked while glancing between them.

Rebekah glanced at him. "Dinner and a movie. A little celebration for finishing the first week of teaching."

He nodded though this time he only looked at Kandice. For a moment, she wondered if she should invite him to come along. After all, it was also his first week at the school. Being alone with Rebekah wasn't necessary.

Liar. The vehemence of that inner voice nearly startled her into jumping.

"Sounds like a damn good date to me. I won't ask you to drop your plans and join some of the other teachers and me at Duffy's to cheer on the weekend." He shrugged. "Maybe next time."

It would be nice to get to meet everyone in a more casual setting, but not after she and Rebekah had already made plans. "Sure. Next time sounds great," Kandice said, hoping that he wouldn't be offended by her not dropping everything to join a teacher outing. "Have a great time at Duffy's."

Robert nodded before passing Rebekah and leaving. Once he was gone, Kandice let out a breath and gave Rebekah a watery smile. "Is it bad that I didn't really want to go?"

Rebekah chuckled and shook her head. "If it is, we're in the same boat. Our old principal never would have invited us out though. As beloved as he was, he was also a real stickler about keeping the professional and personal separate."

Kandice cocked her head as she thought about that. "How was

that really possible? The town is small enough that it would be very hard not to run into someone you weren't at least tangentially connected to on a professional level."

"He lived a couple towns over and the only time I saw him in town was if he was at school or at a school event," Rebekah explained. "Now that he's gone, I doubt I'll ever run into him again."

"See, now that's even weirder to me." Kandice's chest warmed when Rebekah laughed.

"I mean, you're not wrong." Rebekah's smile was wide and open, and it made something in Kandice want to reach out and bath in that warmth.

Get it together. She stood and covered up her thoughts by gathering her things. Her last period of the day was a study period, but a couple students had sat in her room while working on things, so she hadn't been able to really relax. She was ready to get the weekend started off right.

"I'm ready to go if you are," she said once her small bag was packed. She had a couple things to review over the weekend, but thankfully she wouldn't have too much to take home. Not yet, anyway.

Rebekah nodded. "Absolutely. Let's blow this popsicle stand."

Kandice giggled and shook her head. "You have got to stop watching those corny ass movies."

"Hey, they are called classics." She placed a warm hand on Kandice's lower back as they left the room. Kandice tried to ignore how that pressure made her stomach clench as she turned off the lights and closed her door. That small touch made her wonder how it would feel cupping her cheek. *Or somewhere else.* She tried to keep her expression neutral as she let Rebekah lead her from the room and out to their separate cars.

"Why don't you leave yours here and I'll drive?" Rebekah called out when Kandice turned in her car's direction.

"Then you'll have to bring me back."

Rebekah shrugged. "That's fine. I guarantee your car will still be here." She wasn't wrong. Stolen cars weren't really a thing in their town. "Or...you could just crash at mine, and I can bring you in the morning."

The thought of staying at Rebekah's was...something. Or did something. It had static buzzing in Kandice's ears. "Maybe," she murmured noncommittally.

"The place we're going is a couple towns over and the cell service on the way isn't the best, so probably better if we ride together. We could also drop your car at home and then make sure your mom and Caleb are okay with us having a later night."

Kandice only had a split second to think, but she needed the break. She had been holding it all together for a while now and she was ready to have a moment just for her.

"Let's drop my car off at home. I can check with my mom then."

Rebekah's smile was radiant as she nodded. "Sure. I'll meet you at yours." She waited for Kandice to get in her car before pulling out of the parking space.

The drive home was quick, but it still gave Kandice some time to think. Her pulse was racing when she glanced in her rearview mirror and saw Rebekah following. They had been hanging out sporadically since she returned, but tonight somehow felt bigger than before. She was excited, but underneath was a layer of anxiety and restless energy that had her shaking out her hands when she pulled up to a stop sign. By the time she pulled up beside her mom's truck, her nerves were firing, and she hopped out of the car as soon as she had it in park. She heard Rebekah pull in behind her, but was at the front door before Rebekah had even gotten out.

"Ma," Kandice shouted as she opened the front door. Loud footsteps raced down the hallway, and she smiled when Caleb rounded the corner, a golden square of cornbread clutched in his hand.

"Grandma is in the kitchen cooking," he said before taking a large bite. "I thought you were going out with your friend."

Kandice smiled down and ruffled his hair. "I am kiddo. I just came by to—"

"What is with all the yelling?" Margie asked as she came into view. She wiped her hands on the apron around her waist. "Caleb, I know you aren't dropping crumbs in my foyer."

"What's a foyer?" He asked, lips sprinkled with golden yellow crumbs. When he smirked, Margie shook her head before swatting at him with the towel. She chuckled softly as he danced away.

"That boy." She turned to Kandice before her gaze slid behind her. "I thought you two were going to dinner or something."

Kandice glanced over her shoulder when she heard footsteps behind her. Rebekah waved at Margie.

"Evening. We are, but Kandice wanted to drop off her car since we're riding together."

Margie nodded. "Makes sense. Better for you two to travel together anyway. Never know who is out and about at night. It's not as safe here as it was when you two were knee high."

Kandice tried not to say something about how the crime was nothing compared to California. She didn't want to annoy her mom before asking for a favor. "That's another reason I came by. The movie we're going to see starts late. It might be really late when we get out, so I'll probably crash at Rebekah's place if that's okay?"

Margie looked at them both before shrugging. "You're a grown ass woman, so you can do as you see fit."

Not rolling her eyes nearly took all of her strength. "I know, mama. But I wanted to make sure you're okay with staying with Caleb longer. I don't want to interfere with your weekend plans."

"Well, that's nice enough of you to worry about, but I'm fine. You two go have fun and Caleb and I will have our own fun here in the house."

Kandice smiled, relieved that the conversation had gone as

easily as it had. Back when she was younger, it seemed like even small requests started an argument between them. Her ears still rang at the memory of asking her mom to hang out after school with friends instead of coming straight home and doing homework first. Those days, she and her mom had rarely seemed to see eye to eye about anything other than her eventual relationship with Charles. And it was clear how that turned out.

"Great," she said before turning to Rebekah. "I guess we're ready then."

Rebekah smiled and held the front door open. "Guess so. I'll bring her back home safe ma'am."

Margie snorted. "It's not me you have to worry about." She gestured to Caleb who had come back and was standing in the hallway watching with his hands on his hips. "That one would probably take you out before I had a chance to if something happened to his mama."

Rebekah nodded and Kandice felt warmth spread in her chest when she saw the amused yet fond smile on her face. "I promise I'll let no harm come to your mom. Scouts honor."

"You were never a sco—" Kandice started.

"We'll be going now," Rebekah interrupted, guiding her out the door. When Kandice was past her, she closed the door and turned to her. "You can't blow my cover already. Are you trying to get me taken out by your tiny terror?"

Laughter bubbled from her lips as Kandice gave Rebekah a knowing look. "Are you afraid of my ten-year-old? Really?"

"You damn right I am," Rebekah replied without missing a beat. She opened the car door for Kandice. "I've been teaching kids for years and I have seen how fierce some of them get over their moms. I'm not taking any chances."

Amusement filled Kandice as she settled into the seat. Rebekah closed the door before walking around and sitting in the driver's seat. No words were exchanged as she slid on her seatbelt, but at the click of it locking, the two of them looked at one another and that's all it took. The car filled with laughter as they thought about the absurdity of it all. Kandice leaned her head back against the seat and looked over at Rebekah.

"It's been a long while since I've laughed that hard. Thanks."

Rebekah tilted her head in acknowledgement. "Glad I could help. Hopefully this is the first laugh of many." Her brown eyes were warm and the fondness in them hadn't left. It made Kandice's cheeks heat. No one had looked at her like this in a long time. The few months before finding out about Charles' infidelity, he had spent more time working than paying attention to Kandice. Their times together were less filled with laughter and more with the silence that she now could recognize as indifference. She was quickly realizing that she had spent months if not years ignoring the obvious. Her marriage had been crumbling for a long time.

"I hope so too," she said softly before placing a hand on Rebekah's thigh. "I'm glad I came home. I was a little worried at first given how badly Charles used to talk about the town when anybody asked about where he was from."

Rebekah started the car with a wince. "Yeah, I had heard about some of those interviews. He definitely burned some bridges here, but I don't think anyone would take that out on you or Caleb. From what I heard, he's a fan favorite in class with the students and the teachers."

Kandice smiled and looked back at the house. She could imagine Caleb and her mom in the kitchen cooking up their favorites while he chattered a mile a minute. "He really is the best of us. He's taking the impending divorce so well."

"Kids are resilient," Rebekah agreed as she navigated the truck out of the driveway. "You'd be surprised how many bounce back with little to no lasting damage."

Kandice nodded. "I know. It's just hard not to see it as failing him. Things weren't perfect but before finding out about the cheating, I thought we would still be fine, and it was just a rough patch." She sighed. "I spent so much time just being a wife and mom that I'm finding I don't know what to do with myself now."

They were quiet for a moment, the only sounds coming from the tires on the road and the wind whistling past the trees. Kandice knew she had dropped some heavy information, and she wondered if maybe it was too much too soon. She and Rebekah had only connected a couple weeks ago and already she was dumping her trauma all over the place. She clenched her fists and looked out the window.

"I think you do this," Rebekah finally said, her voice gone deeper as it always did when she was being serious. The sound of it used to annoy Kandice when they were kids, but she was having a far more different reaction to it now. It made her want to sit up and listen. Rebekah glanced at her. "Get out of the house. Make new friends and find hobbies that bring you joy. I won't pretend to know what it's like, but I know you are a mom and so much more. There's nothing wrong with figuring out what you want for yourself and then working towards that."

Kandice stared. It's the same words that had been repeating in her own mind, but hearing someone else say them made her feel like she really could.

Chapter 6

REBEKAH

"I might have overestimated my stomach's capacity."

Rebekah laughed as she settled into her seat. Dinner had been delicious as expected and the conversation had flowed with no awkwardness. It was amazing how well the two of them seemed to settle into the same easy friendship that they had more than a decade ago. She had wondered if they would run out of things to talk about, but between talking about living in California and everything that had happened since their high school graduation, there was never a moment of silence even with steering away from questions about their friendship breakdown.

"I told you ordering that appetizer would come back to bite you in the butt," she replied with a grin.

Kandice shifted until she seemed to find a comfortable position in her theater chair. "It's not my butt I'm worried about." Her smile was wide when Rebekah laughed again. "I don't understand how you can eat dinner and order popcorn and still look that good. If I even smell butter, I swear I gain five pounds."

She thinks I look good? That was all Rebekah heard, but she kicked her brain into catching up so she didn't let the conversation lull. "I'm still an everyday runner. After mom passed, I converted one of the spare rooms in the house into a mini gym. You're more than welcome to come work out with me." *In more ways than one.* She pushed that thought away. Things were going so well. Now was not the time to have inappropriate thoughts. "There's been talk about a gym being opened in town, but so far I think it's still just a rumor."

Kandice shook her head. "Running on a treadmill is not my idea of fun."

"I have other things," Rebekah reassured her. "Running is only one way to work out."

"What would you suggest I do then?"

"Well..." Her voice trailed off as she looked at Kandice. The other woman had leaned her head back on the headrest, rolling it to look at her. That left her neck stretched and bare for Rebekah's greedy eyes. She gazed over that skin wondering how it would feel if she brushed her lips against it. She slowly dragged her eyes up to meet Kandice's and hers widened when she thought she saw something there. There was *heat.* She was sure of it. She could recognize it as the same look she had in her own eyes when she looked in the mirror this morning as she thought about spending time with Kandice this evening. Thankfully, the lights dimming saved her from having to come up with anything. They both turned to the screen and settled in for the next couple hours.

It only took a few minutes of the movie starting for Rebekah to realize they had made a terrible mistake in their choice of movie. Watching a romantic comedy might have seemed like an innocent way of passing the time, until the kissing happened. She tried to ignore Kandice's warmth as it soaked into her side. They had both leaned into one another but it wasn't until their fingers brushed as Rebekah reached for popcorn that the buzzing in her mind cut off abruptly. Rebekah turned to glance at Kandice only to realize she was already looking back.

The screen illuminated the side of Kandice's face and made her eyes seem bigger, drawing Rebekah in before she even realized what she was doing. When their lips met, it was like a sparkler had gone off in front of her. She couldn't help the way her eyes slid shut and the soft noise of pleasure from the joining of their lips.

As far as kisses went, Rebekah had had plenty, but none before had ever felt so consuming. It was as if every nerve in her body was connected to where the skin of her lips met Kandice's. She brought a hand up to cup Kandice's cheek without stopping to consider where they were. The theater wasn't packed, but they definitely weren't alone. Anyone could look over and see them kissing, and yet that didn't dissuade Rebekah in the slightest. Her hand shifted from Kandice's cheek to the back of her neck, gripping tight and bringing their lips more firmly together. It brought a new dimension to the kiss that had Rebekah moaning. As soon as her lips parted, Kandice's tongue darted in. It swept through laying siege to the last tendrils of Rebekah's control as her body clenched with the need for *more*. It wasn't until a booming noise came from the screen that she finally gathered the strength to pull back.

Kandice's eyes opened slowly as if coming out of a dream. "What?" Her voice was gravelly and deeper, scraping something in Rebekah that had her hand clenching where it still curved around the back of Kandice's neck. The resulting flutter of Kandice's eyes nearly had her leaning in again. "What the hell was that?"

The question seemed more than a little ridiculous considering. "That was a kiss."

"Don't be a smartass." Kandice hissed softly. Though there was no bite in her words, they still had Rebekah withdrawing further. "You kissed me. Why did you kiss me?"

Why did she kiss her? That was a question Rebekah absolutely had an answer for, she just wasn't sure if the answer would be appreciated. Because truthfully, she had been wanting to kiss Kandice damn near since the moment she saw her in town again. That was the truth of it. Her feelings, those annoying things she thought long faded away after the time and space between them, had come surging back as if just waiting for a spark to ignite them.

"Why not?" Rebekah whispered.

"Because," Kandice sputtered out, her volume rising slightly before she looked back at the screen and seemed to remember where they were. "I'm not..."

"You're not what? Gay? Interested?" Now, Rebekah felt the embers of anger wanting to strike a match. She had to swallow hard to lower her voice with her next words. "Are you still trying to hide behind the label of straight girls who kiss their friends all the time?"

She saw Kandice clench her fists. She was expecting a fight, but that isn't what she got. By the time her brain kicked in, Kandice had hopped out of her seat and was striding down the stairs and towards the exit. Rebekah blinked slowly before she jumped up to follow. By the time she caught up, Kandice was outside and headed towards the car.

"Kandice, wait!" Rebekah hurried after her. They reached the car at the same time, and she put her hand on the passenger door to stop Kandice from getting in. "Just wait. Talk to me, please."

Kandice turned to her, expression looking unamused about being stopped. "Oh, now you're asking and being polite."

"I was polite before," Rebekah replied. She put her hands up before Kandice could say something else. "No, listen. I wasn't trying to piss you off. You just looked pretty in the light, and I clearly mistook things."

"Yes, you did."

"But also, you need to ask yourself," she said, ignoring Kandice's words. "What does it mean that you kissed me back?"

That clearly surprised Kandice because she didn't respond right away. She took a step back as her lips flattened into a thin line. Rather than say anything else, Rebekah unlocked the door and opened it. She didn't bother waiting, instead she walked around the car and got in. Kandice paused for a moment longer before also getting in. The car was silent save the click of their seatbelts and the rumble of the engine. When Rebekah pulled out of the lot, she sighed and prepared herself for the longest drive home.

Focusing on the drive didn't stop her mind from racing. She had clearly made a terrible miscalculation, but she knew she couldn't leave things the way they were. By the time she pulled up to Kandice's mom's house, she had finally come up with a way to start the conversation they should have had as soon as they started hanging out again.

"Listen," she said after putting the car in park. "I think we need to talk about things so everything can get out into the open."

Kandice crossed her arms. "I don't think there's anything to talk about."

The steering wheel creaked as Rebekah tightened her grip. "Are we doing this again? Are you going to pretend like nothing happened and then stop all communication? You know, I thought before that you not reaching out was all Charles' doing, but I'm starting to wonder if I was fooling myself."

Kandice's head whirled around at the accusation. "I didn't disappear, Rebekah. We both left for college and life just got busy with classes and Charles' football. Plus, it's not like you tried very hard to keep in touch with me." Her voice turned hard and her accusation that it was Rebekah at fault nearly had her reeling away.

Does she really think our contact just faded away because of a couple weeks of being busy? The thought had Rebekah scoffing. "Are you seriously going to act like you don't know why I stopped calling? We were best friends for years—"

"Apparently not if your jealousy made you stop reaching out."

"Jealousy?" Rebekah could hear the hysterical edge to her voice, but she was in it too far now to stop where this conversation was inevitably leading too. "What the hell are you talking about?"

Kandice clenched her jaw before speaking. "Yes, jealousy. Riley let it slip after she saw how upset I was about you ignoring me. She told me how you reacted to Charles and I the last time you came to visit me at college. How you turned your nose up and acted like—"

"Riley?" Rebekah couldn't help but interrupt. "The same Riley who fucked your husband? You're trusting what she said instead of just talking to me?"

"You didn't give me much of a choice."

Rebekah opened her mouth, but nothing came out then. This entire conversation was absurd. This was not how she wanted to discuss things and yet here they were, arguing about shit that should have been squashed years ago. It was almost laughable how even now that they were back face-to-face they were still so far apart. With a sigh, Rebekah loosened her grip on the steering wheel.

"I was never jealous of you for being with Charles, Kandice. I was jealous of *him* for being with *you*." The silence that met her spoke volumes. It drove Rebekah from the car. Before she even realized what she was doing, she had Kandice's door open. "I don't know what they said to you to make you think so lowly of me, but all I wanted was to be your friend. No, that's a lie."

Kandice stepped out of the car, her gaze still stuck on Rebekah. Rebekah didn't want to meet those eyes, but she forced herself to. It was time to get everything out and let things fall wherever they would.

"Rebekah, I..."

"It's fine," she said, cutting Kandice off. She wasn't ready to hear whatever apology she had ready. "I think we should cut the rest of the night short and think about things."

Before Kandice could say anything else, Rebekah closed the car door. She walked back around and got in her seat. She knew it might be rude, but she didn't wait for Kandice to say anything before pulling away. The night had started so promising but now she felt worse than ever before.

Chapter 7

KANDICE

K andice groaned as she turned over in bed. The sun was too damn bright to fit with her shitty mood. Last night had not ended well and she was even more sure in the light of a new day that it was mostly her fault.

"I was never jealous of you for being with Charles, Kandice. I was jealous of him for being with you."

Rebekah's words had stayed with her even after the lights from her car had long since faded away into the dark. Like a robot, Kandice had walked into the house, vaguely noting that it was quieter than she had expected it to be. She hadn't paused before walking into her room and falling into bed. Sleep hadn't come easy and by the time she finally drifted off, she had a half-formed apology ready to go. Now though, she wasn't so sure if she should reach out or not.

It had been years since she was this unsure about someone. Even when dealing with Charles, she had never been this unsure. Delusional maybe. She had to have been to think their relationship was anything other than a farce. It had taken infidelity to make her feel half as much with him as she did from this small argument with Rebekah. Then again...was it really small?

"Fuck," she muttered, scrubbing a hand over her face. She sighed when she saw the dark smudges of mascara on her palm. She had forgotten that she didn't wash her face before crashing, something she would no doubt be paying for if the smudges on her hands were any indication. A knock on the door grabbed her attention and she called out for the person to enter. She smiled when she saw it was Caleb.

"Hey kiddo. You're up early." He walked over to the bed, sitting down when she gestured to him. Kandice gave him a hug, smiling when he allowed it. These days, he sometimes didn't want to move into her embrace as readily as he used to. She always let it go, but sometimes it was a hard pill to swallow that he was growing up

"Grandma says to get your butt out of bed and come down for breakfast." He grinned when she raised an eyebrow. "Those were her words, not mine. I'm just telling you what she said."

"Is that so?" Kandice teased. She didn't doubt it. "Grandma is about to get you in some trouble."

Before he could move, she tickled his sides enjoying the loud whoop of laughter that resulted. They struggled for a minute before they both relaxed back on the bed.

"Did you have fun last night with Ms. Rebekah?"

"I did." She cocked her head at him. "Did you and grandma have a good night?"

Caleb shrugged. "Yeah. We cooked and talked before she let me play my game on the big tv. She told me you and Ms. Rebekah were friends when you were kids."

Kandice nodded slowly. "Did she tell you anything else?"

"Like what?" He wrinkled his brow in clear confusion. Kandice wasn't even sure why she was pressing. It's not like there was anything going on between her and Rebekah anyway. *Not anymore.* That inner voice pushed her out of bed instead of answering, and she pulled Caleb up as well so they could head downstairs. When they reached the landing, Kandice caught the faint scent of bacon frying. By the time they walked into the kitchen, her mouth was watering and her stomach growling at the scents that assaulted her. There was bacon and biscuits, but they were also joined by fried eggs and coffee.

"This looks good mama," Kandice said appreciatively. "Do you need help with anything?"

Margie gestured to the cabinets. "If you could take us out some plates, that would be fine." Kandice moved to do that.

When the table was set and the food placed around in easy reach, Kandice sighed softly. She had hoped to catch an early or late bite with Rebekah yesterday, but things clearly hadn't panned out, something Margie was quick to point out.

"I thought you were staying at Rebekah's last night."

Kandice scooped out some eggs on Caleb's plate, not looking at her mother. "Yeah, well...things didn't plan out the way I had hoped." She had hoped her mom would leave it at that, but Kandice was quickly realizing that maybe she should start hoping for the opposite of what she really wanted.

"That's unfortunate," Margie said. "She could be a good influence on you."

"I'm almost thirty, mom. I don't need someone else to be a good influence on me," Kandice replied with a roll of her eyes. "Besides, weren't you the one telling me to think for myself and not follow after her back when she and I were younger?"

Margie waved a hand dismissing her words. "That was so long ago. Don't tell me you're still hung up on all that?"

"Hung up?" Kandice nearly yelled before she pulled herself back. Caleb was at the table and even though he had headphones on, she didn't doubt he was occasionally listening in on their conversation. She didn't want to argue in front of him. She closed her eyes and took a deep breath before speaking again. "I distinctly remember you telling me how worried you were about my relationship with Rebekah to the point that you and pa actively tried to keep me from seeing her."

She knew her words had hit their mark when her mother looked away. Her face was pinched with an uncomfortable expression. It was then Kandice knew there was a lot more to get out into the open than she had originally thought. With another sigh, she tapped Caleb's arm to get his attention.

"Caleb, honey. Why don't you go watch cartoons in the living room."

He snorted. "You and grandma just don't want me listening to your conversation."

Margie clicked her tongue at him. "Boy, go on into the living room like your mama asked." He grumbled before getting up with his plate. "And make sure you don't spill nothing on my carpet."

"Yes ma'am."

Kandice watched him shuffle from the room, his plate and cup in his hands. A few seconds later, she heard the television turn on and the hum of conversation. Only then did she turn back to her mom.

"So, explain to me why you all of a sudden are singing Rebekah's praises," Kandice demanded, leaning back in her seat and crossing her arms. Margie pursed her lips.

"It's not all of a sudden," she denied. When Kandice raised an eyebrow, she continued, "I have never said Rebekah was a bad person."

"You never said she was a good person either," Kandice pointed out. "Whenever Charles came back home to visit, you and pa acted like me hanging out with Rebekah was a problem. And even when he wasn't around—"

"It's not that we didn't want you two to hang out," Margie interrupted. "It's that I knew she wasn't what you needed for your future."

Her words lit a fire within Kandice, and she leaned forward with her next words. "That wasn't your choice to make. It was mine." Words that had been stuck in her throat suddenly came tumbling out and she almost tumbled with them. "She was my best friend and then she just wasn't." Thoughts and feelings long buried suddenly bubbled up from the cracks inside her. Before she could say anything else, her mom surprised the hell out of her.

"I think you need to talk to Rebekah and tell her how you feel."

"...Wait, what?"

"You heard me," Margie replied. At the look on Kandice's face, she sighed. "I don't know why you're acting all surprised."

"Because I am," Kandice insisted. She dropped her hands in her lap as she tried to come up with words to say. Had she somehow wound up in a different dimension. "Explain to me why you've had this change in feelings, because you can't lie to me and say you always felt this way."

Margie paused for a moment, fork in hand as she looked down at her plate. When she spoke again, her voice was abnormally subdued. "Did you know I almost divorced your father?"

Kandice frowned. "What? When?"

"Which time do you want me to mention?" Her smile didn't reach her eyes as she looked up at Kandice. There was pain there—a familiar pain and it made Kandice's breath hitch and her chest ache. Margie nodded in understanding. "Yes. A couple years before your daddy died, I found out he was stepping out. Told me he would change. That same old song and dance, but he never did. And that was just the first time I let him know that I knew."

An ache, deep and powerful lanced through Kandice. "Why didn't you ever say anything?"

"Because you didn't need to know," Margie replied. When Kandice disagreed, she shook her head. "You were a kid, baby. You didn't need to know that your daddy was anything but a good father to you. And I wanted you to focus on your future. If I had left your father then, with no job and no way to support us, you would have wound up like some of the girls around here. Pregnant before the ink was even dry on your degree. I wanted more for you."

Kandice shook her head slowly still not understanding what this had to do with Rebekah. "I don't understand."

"Honey, at the time, all Rebekah talked about was moving to Los Angeles and trying to do music. That wasn't a stable career. That wasn't a sure future." At that, her voice took on an almost pleading tone. "Charles was years ahead of you both, and already was looking to sign a deal to play professional ball. He had the means to take care of you."

"He put me in a cage," Kandice said forcefully. Only, when the words were out, she realized they weren't quite true. Yes, they accelerated their relationship when she got pregnant her freshman year of college, but she still could have made different choices. She could have chosen to go after what she really wanted.

"No," Kandice said after a moment of reflection. "I put myself in a cage. I lost myself in being a wife and mother and I pushed away the one person who had always told me I could be more."

"Was it really that bad, honey?"

Kandice snorted. "I'm divorced mom."

"Right. Well..." Her voice trailed off as they sat in silence, the only sounds filtering between them coming from the living room television. "I'm sorry."

Kandice looked up in surprise. When Margie saw her expression, she chuckled and shook her head. "I do know how to apologize. I don't know why you look so damn surprised."

"Mama, I can count on one hand the number of times you've apologized to me in our entire relationship." Kandice smiled softly, letting her off the hook. "But thank you. I do appreciate it."

"Yes, well I saw how Rebekah took care of her mama when she got sick," Margie explained. "She didn't hesitate to come back and even after her mama passed, she stayed and started working with the kids. Teaching is sometimes such a thankless job and I know how hard it is to inspire children to want to do anything but laze around all day."

Kandice rolled her eyes. "And we are back to the nagging."

"Oh poo," Margie said before picking up her fork. She stabbed a piece of egg but paused before eating it. "Listen here, child. I know it's terrifying trying again after you get burned so badly. But you should talk to her. Be honest about your feelings instead of taking the easy way out and running from them."

Kandice rubbed her eyes as if that would help sort out the madness she was hearing. "I don't understand, mama. Are you seriously telling me that I should be with Rebekah? Like as in be in a relationship with her?"

"If it's what you want and what she wants, then yes. Life is too damn short to waste time worrying." She paused and gazed out the dining room window. "Otherwise, one day you might wake up and realize life has gone by and left you behind."

Curiosity burned a hole in her chest as Kandice wondered what the story there was. Was there someone her mom had wished she had chosen instead? Margie spoke again before she could ask.

"Talk to Rebekah. Straighten everything out. Don't live with regrets."

Kandice swallowed hard but nodded. She would call Rebekah. She could only hope that she hadn't burned that bridge one too many times.

Chapter 8

REBEKAH

Rebekah curled her legs beneath her on the couch, an old, soft blanket draped around her shoulders like a shield. The afternoon sun bled lazily through the half-closed blinds, painting pale gold stripes across her living room. Her tea had long gone cold on the side table, untouched since she'd poured it an hour ago. Her thoughts, chaotic and looping endlessly, refused to give her peace even after she had exhausted her usual methods of working out and reading.

She couldn't stop replaying last night in her mind, scene after awkward scene with her and Kandice at the center. The tension between them when they had walked in, already carrying years of unspoken words between them. The way Kandice had laughed at something stupid on screen, and how Rebekah had felt her heart twist at that same familiar laugh that still lit her up inside.

And that kiss.

She exhaled sharply and pressed a palm to her forehead as a wave of warmth spread through her. It wasn't just a mistake—it was a gut punch. It had felt like surrendering, like admitting something she'd buried so deep she could barely look at it straight. A whisper of something that had never been just friendship. She had been content to lie to herself until then.

A knock at the front door broke through her spiraling and Rebekah sighed and stood, letting the blanket fall from her shoulders. When she opened the door, Emma stood there with coffees in her hands and a knowing look in her eyes.

"I brought backup," Emma said with a small smile, holding the drink out like a peace offering.

"You're a saint," Rebekah muttered, taking the coffee and stepping aside to let her in. Emma walked in snorting and gesturing at the half-open blinds.

"I figured you'd be in a state today. You never texted back last night." She arched an eyebrow at Rebekah before immediately making herself at home on the couch.

"I was...processing," Rebekah said, sinking back onto the couch and clutching the warm cup like it could anchor her. "Oh, who the fuck am I kidding. Last night was a fucking disaster."

Emma raised both eyebrows at her wording. "Define disaster."

Rebekah gave a mirthless laugh. "You want the short version or the emotionally gutting one?"

"I brought caffeine. Give me the gutting."

Rebekah hesitated, staring down at her cup. Saying it all out loud would make it real, but she had been sitting alone all morning with the weight of her thoughts. Maybe passing some of that to someone else would help her untangle the web that had been weaved.

"It was a mess from the moment we sat down. We haven't spoken in, what, almost ten years? And now suddenly we're at the movies like we're in high school again and things are just like they had always been before it all turned to shit. Except it's not. There's all this...stuff between us. And then I went and kissed her like an idiot."

Emma nodded, quietly encouraging.

Rebekah sighed. "We didn't even talk. Not really. Not about

the big things. I mean, we caught up a little and exchanged a few jokes here and there, but it was all surface level, like we were afraid to go deeper."

"But you kissed," Emma said, not a question.

Rebekah flinched slightly. "Yeah. It just...happened. And I hate that it felt so familiar. Like my heart still thinks we belong to each other."

Emma was quiet for a moment. "What exactly happened between you two? You would talk about her sometimes and just vaguely mention that you two lost touch, but it always felt like I shouldn't push for details."

"It's complicated I guess."

"Or maybe it isn't, and you've gotten used to getting in your own way." When Rebekah narrowed her eyes, Emma put her hands up. "Hey, don't shoot the messenger. I'm just trying to help you get to the bottom of this so you can either woman up and declare you belong together or move the fuck on so I can set you up with my cousin Deirdre. She told me after her last visit that she thought you were super cute."

Rebekah chuckled and shook her head. Her smile fell as she hesitated. Her chest tightened, the old ache of the breakdown of Kandice and her friendship waking up as if summoned.

"I guess it all started when Kandice and Charles hooked up our senior year when he was back in town to visit," she said finally. "He was from Hickory Springs, but he always thought he was hot shit and better than everyone in town. Still, they propped him up like some golden boy. It always pissed me off how no one saw how much of an ass he was."

Emma snorted but gestured for Rebekah to continue.

"At first, I was happy for Kandice. She seemed to really like him and even though I didn't like him, I kept it quiet. It wasn't until spring of our senior year when I realized he didn't like me either."

That had Emma frowning. "Really? You always seem to get along with everyone."

Rebekah shrugged before taking a sip of her coffee. She winced at the heat. "I don't know. Maybe it was because I saw through his bullshit. He was always so...controlling, in subtle ways. Making her feel guilty for going out or for needing space. The summer before college, every time Kandice and I made plans, she'd cancel last minute. He'd make her feel like she was abandoning him even though he was away. Even when we started college and we'd only get to talk maybe once a week, he still gave her shit about it."

Emma hummed thoughtfully before lifting her own cup to her lips. "Sounds like classic isolation tactics to me."

Rebekah blinked. "What?"

"You said he didn't like you. That he made her feel guilty for seeing you. That's isolating behavior, 'Bekah."

Rebekah opened her mouth, then closed it. "I guess I never thought about it like that. I just figured he didn't want her to be around me so much because he knew she and I used to have a thing. Like he was afraid Kandice would cheat with me or some-thing. Which we never did or would. Kandice and I agreed that our friendship was too important to mess up by risking a relationship."

"I'm not even going to touch on how nonsensical that sounds, but his behavior seems clear to me. People like that want control. And friends, regardless of anything else between you, were a threat to that."

Rebekah sat back, the realization slamming into her harder than she expected. "Wow. It all makes sense now. Riley had to be in on it then."

Emma gave her a moment before continuing. "Who?"

Rebekah shook her head. "One of Kandice's friends from college. Or I guess frenemy is a better description considering she ended up fucking Charles which is why Kandice is even back home in the first place."

Emma coughed, a choking hack that brought a small smile to Rebekah's face. She glared when Rebekah slapped her on the back. "You didn't mention that part."

"I mean, I hadn't gotten there yet," Rebekah said with a shrug. "Riley started telling people I was jealous of Kandice. That I wanted her life, her relationship. She even insinuated once that I had feelings for Charles. Never mind that I'm a lesbian. It was all so ridiculous now that I think about it."

Emma grimaced. "Ew." She shook her head.

"I know," Rebekah said, letting out a bitter laugh. "Like I would ever. But Kandice believed it. Or at least, she never asked me about it. She just started pulling away more. And then one day, she stopped answering my texts. That was it. Just...silence."

"Damn," Emma said, her voice soft. "She should've known you better than that."

"I thought she did." Rebekah looked down at her hands. "But maybe I didn't know her either."

A long silence stretched between them, broken only by the hum of the refrigerator in the kitchen and the muted sounds of birds outside the window. Then Emma said quietly, "Do you think maybe she was hurting too? That maybe she didn't know how to come back from it all?"

Rebekah didn't answer right away. Her mind drifted back to last night again—the way Kandice had looked at her after the kiss. Not confused. Not angry. Just...sad.

"She didn't seem happy," Rebekah said. "Even when she smiled. It felt forced."

Emma nodded. "Maybe she regrets what happened. Maybe she just doesn't know how to say it."

Rebekah took a shaky breath. "Part of me still loves her, Emma. And I don't even know what kind of love it is anymore. Friendship? Something more? It all feels so tangled up."

Emma leaned forward; her voice gentle but firm. "Then talk to her. Get everything out in the open. You two work together. This isn't going to just disappear. Better to know where you stand than to keep torturing yourself."

"What if it ends badly?" Rebekah whispered.

"Then at least you'll know. And you can finally close the chapter, like you said. But maybe—just maybe—it won't end badly. Maybe she's been waiting for a chance to make things right too."

Rebekah looked at her friend, the warmth and patience in her eyes, and felt a wave of gratitude.

"I'm scared," she admitted. "What if we can't figure this shit out, you know? I don't even know if she's planning on staying here for good. I used to think about leaving and heading back to Los Angeles and trying again, or making my way to Nashville like I planned back then, but I'm happy here."

"You won't know until you try, friend," Emma said. "But you've faced scarier things than a conversation. You could be driving in L.A. during rush hour."

Rebekah shivered at the memory. "Well, when you put it that way." Emma's laughter made something loosen in Rebekah's chest. "I'll talk to her. Anything is better than this limbo. This is worse than dealing with Susan."

Emma screwed her nose up. "Don't even mention that woman's name in my presence. If I see her again, I might have to knock some sense into her myself."

Rebekah laughed as Emma stood and followed to walk her out. When the door closed behind her, Rebekah sat in the quiet for a long time. Her fingers hovered over her phone, heart pounding. But this time, she wasn't drowning in what-ifs.

She was ready for answers.

Chapter 9

KANDICE

It had been three days since the kiss. Three days since the dim flicker of the movie theater and the sharp press of lips that had left Kandice with a hunger she hadn't known she could feel. The fight that had followed, like thunder chasing lightning, had been the reason she found herself still trying to think about how to start the conversation she knew was needed. She had promised herself she would reach out and talk to Rebekah to fix this tangled mess between them, and yet she hadn't. She'd continued to run like always.

Kandice sighed as she looked around her now-empty classroom, the fluorescent lights humming faintly above her. The last bell had rung thirty minutes ago, and she was sure most of the teachers were long gone no doubt headed to happy hour that was quickly becoming a Tuesday evening norm. Caleb had waved as he ran by on his way to the bus. He'd been excited on their drive to school, chattering all about Margie taking him to the apple orchard after she picked him up from the bus stop. Kandice wished she was going instead of doing admin work. She stared blankly at her computer screen, pretending to grade, though her eyes weren't tracking the words. Her heart wasn't in it—not today. Not this week.

She had chickened out.

Every time she pulled out her phone and opened the messages, her fingers hovered above Rebekah's name like it burned her. What was she supposed to say?

Sorry I kissed you and then freaked out? Sorry I let you believe I didn't want to be friends anymore.

Sorry I let you think I didn't feel anything when it nearly tore me apart?

The classroom door creaked open, snapping her from her spiral and she looked up, hope warming her chest. She tried not to let her smile slip when she saw Robert standing there. His tall frame filled the doorway, and as always, he wore his easy-going smile like a mask he'd long since forgotten how to remove.

"Hey, Kandice," he said, strolling in without invitation. "I'm surprised you're still here. Didn't you get the invite for the teacher happy hour?"

"Yeah," she said, sitting up straighter. "Just finishing up some grading."

He nodded, resting a hand on the back of a student's chair. "Listen, you should come. Blow off some steam and get to know your colleagues in a less tense setting."

Kandice hesitated. "I don't know. I've got some things to—"

"Oh, come on," he interrupted, grinning wider. "You've earned it. Plus, everyone's going. It's a good morale boost, even if you don't want to drink more than a coke."

She could hear the eagerness under his tone, a little too enthusiastic for a casual work hangout. It made her skin itch in a way she couldn't fully explain. Still, the idea of heading home and dealing with the same looping regret while under her mom's knowing gaze wasn't exactly inviting.

"Okay," she said, reluctantly. "Sure. I'll join everyone for a little while."

"Great," Robert said, too quickly. "I'll see you there." He turned and left, whistling a little tune as he disappeared down the hall.

Kandice packed up her bag slowly, already second-guessing her decision. But a part of her—small, fragile, but stubborn—hoped maybe Rebekah would be there. Maybe this was the push she needed. Maybe fate was tired of waiting on them to sort themselves out.

THE BAR on Main Street was already humming with post-work laughter and the low rumble of conversations when Kandice arrived. Warm light spilled out of the windows, and through the glass, she could see a few familiar faces gathered near the corner booths.

Kandice paused at the door, adjusting the strap of her bag on her shoulder. Then she took a deep breath and stepped inside. The scent of beer and fried food hit her first, followed by the laughter of someone she vaguely recognized from the fifth-grade team. She scanned the room, heart thudding harder than it had any right to. It nearly came to a stop when she finally saw Rebekah.

She was sitting near the back wall with Justin—a kind, funny PE teacher Kandice had spoken to once or twice in the break room. Rebekah's head was tilted toward him as she laughed at something he'd said, her face glowing in the golden pub light and Kandice's chest constricted. Before she could move, or escape back out the door, Robert appeared beside her with a drink already in hand.

"There you are," he said, gesturing toward the back. "Come on, we've got a seat for you." Before she could protest, he was already leading her toward Rebekah's table. Rebekah glanced up just as Kandice approached, and their eyes met for the first time in three days. The moment hung there, heavy and charged, before Justin smiled and scooted over.

"Hey," Justin said cheerfully, clearly unaware of the tension brewing. "Sit with us."

Kandice sat, feeling awkward and off-balance, and took the beer Robert handed her. Rebekah gave a small nod, her expression unreadable, before she looked away.

The conversation swirled around her—Justin talking about his latest classroom chaos, Robert chiming in with a joke or two—but Kandice couldn't focus. Her eyes kept drifting to Rebekah. She was quiet, only occasionally jumping in to comment or laugh, but her body language was closed, tense. Like she was holding something back.

And then Rebekah stood.

"I'm going to grab another drink," she said casually, slipping off her stool.

Kandice watched her weave through the crowd, saw the way her posture changed when a woman with shoulder-length auburn hair intercepted her near the bar. The woman leaned in, familiar and easy, and Rebekah didn't pull away. Kandice felt her stomach drop as the two shared a laugh, the woman touching Rebekah's arm, her hand lingering a second too long.

Who is she?

Kandice hated the jealousy that flared lava hot in her chest. She knew it was an irrational feeling to have. She had no more claim on Rebekah than the other woman had on her, and yet she couldn't help the emotions that swirled in her. She took a long sip of her beer, trying to ignore it, but the taste was bitter and metallic on her tongue.

"I'll be right back," she muttered and slipped from the table.

The bathroom was tucked down a narrow hallway near the back that was cool, and dim compared to the warm bustle of the pub. Kandice leaned over the sink, staring into the mirror. Her reflection looked tired in a way it hadn't in a while. Sure, her ongoing divorce was stressful, but with most of the arrangements agreed upon, that was more of just a waiting game. This though—this was a whole new brand of stress that dug in deep and refused to let go.

You're not even together, she told herself fiercely. *You don't get to feel this.*

With a sigh, she washed her hands and pushed open the door to head back to the table.

"Kandice," came Robert's voice, and she nearly jumped. He was leaning against the wall across from the bathroom, his expression casual but his eyes focused on her. "Is everything okay? You left kind of abruptly." he asked.

"Oh, I'm fine," she said shortly as she let the door close behind her. "Just needed a break."

Robert stepped closer. "You know, I was thinking...maybe you and I could grab a drink sometime. Just the two of us."

Kandice blinked. "What?"

He shrugged, too nonchalant. "We've worked together for a couple weeks now and yet I feel like I haven't gotten to know you as much as the others."

The air grew cold around her. "Robert...I'm flattered, but I don't think that's a good idea."

Something flickered across his face—surprise, then mild irritation. He covered it quickly with a practiced smile. "No problem. Just figured I'd ask."

She gave a tight nod and brushed past him. She could feel his eyes on her as she rounded the corner of the hallway, but her attention was stolen when she walked right into Rebekah. They stopped short, inches apart.

"Hey," Rebekah said, her voice low, uncertain.

"Hey," Kandice replied, heart pounding all over again. There was a long pause. The kind that vibrated with everything unsaid.

"Listen, I think we should talk. Is now a good time?" Rebekah asked finally. "We could go outside?"

Kandice hesitated, then nodded. "Yeah." She followed Rebekah out, nodding in thanks when she held the door open letting Kandice walk out first. They stepped out into the night air, the door clicking shut behind them. The sun was quickly dipping below the horizon bringing the night a little sooner each day. The parking lot was quiet, distant music leaking from inside. A breeze tugged gently at Kandice's sleeves. She shivered slightly before folding her arms.

They walked down the sidewalk to keep from blocking the door though Kandice had even more reason for it. She didn't want everyone in the bar to bear witness to her silent freak out while she tried to think of everything she needed to say. She paused by one of the streetlamps. Rebekah stood beside her for a moment before turning to face her.

"I'm sorry," she said, wanting to make sure she said those words out loud. Rebekah looked at her for a moment before speaking.

"You didn't reach out."

"I know," Kandice said softly. "I should have. I wanted to. I just didn't know what to say to explain how I was feeling. I still don't, maybe."

She looked up at Rebekah's steady gaze. She could see the hurt there and she knew it wasn't just for what happened between them a couple days ago. "You kissed me. Then you pulled away like it didn't mean anything."

"It did mean something," Kandice said quickly, her voice breaking. "That's why I pulled away. Because it scared the hell out of me the way nothing else ever has."

Rebekah looked away, her jaw tight. "You think it didn't scare me too?"

Kandice took a deep breath. "It's not just about the kiss, Rebekah. It's everything. All the things we never talked about. Charles. Riley. The way everything fell apart."

"You think I don't remember?" Rebekah's voice rose. "You

think I haven't spent the last ten years wondering what I did wrong? How I lost my best friend without even a conversation?"

"You didn't do anything wrong," Kandice whispered. "I shouldn't have listened to Charles when he said you were getting in the way of our relationship. You weren't and you wouldn't have even tried. You always were so supportive even if deep down I knew he didn't deserve it."

Rebekah huffed out a breath. "He knew I didn't like him." Kandice hesitated before nodding. Rebekah's lips quirked up, but it looked more like a grimace than a smile. "Emma helped me realize a few things. Namely that he was isolating you."

Kandice sucked in a sharp breath. She had slowly begun to suspect something similar, but hearing Rebekah say the words out loud broke something apart in her chest and there it was, clear as a perfect summer day for all to see.

"You didn't realize it...did you?"

She shook her head before looking down. "Not until recently. But it still doesn't change the fact that I was horrible to you. He might have had a hand in that, but at the end of the day, you were the only one who ever really saw me—who believed and encouraged me in whatever I wanted, and I let you go because it was easier than facing the truth."

Rebekah turned to her fully now, eyes wide. "What are you saying?"

Kandice stepped closer, voice trembling. "I think I buried how I felt because I thought it wasn't allowed. I convinced myself it was just friendship because it wasn't what I was supposed to do. Because *you* weren't who I was supposed to be with even if that was what I wanted."

"Kandice—"

"No," she said, cutting Rebekah off. "I need to say this, because you never pressed. I listened to everyone but you. I let people push you away. I let *me* push you away when all I really wanted was to keep you close."

Rebekah's expression cracked, pain and hope colliding in her eyes.

"I'm sorry," Kandice whispered. "For all of it. I'm sorry for pushing you away and I'm sorry for not trying to fix things sooner. I'm so sorry."

Rebekah reached up, cupping her cheek. "Thank you," she said just as softly. Her voice was full of emotion, and it almost had Kandice losing it right there on the sidewalk regardless of who might have walked by. "I'm sorry too for not trying harder."

Kandice shook her head before curling a hand around Rebekah's. "No. You don't get to apologize because you did nothing wrong."

The ghost of a smile on Rebekah's lips had Kandice's heart thumping loud enough she was surprised it didn't echo down the street. "I don't know where this leaves us."

"I don't either," Kandice said. "But maybe we could...try again?"

"Our friendship?"

Kandice swallowed hard before taking a leap. "Or maybe...as something more?"

There was a long beat of silence, and she almost took her words back. It was on her tongue to make a joke out of it and try to diffuse the seriousness of the situation, but Kandice refused to spend more time not going for what she wanted. After a moment, Rebekah nodded, slow and cautious.

"Okay. Something more." The smile that spread across her face was like the coming of dawn, wonderous and beautiful. Kandice's breath caught and she didn't even want it back. She wanted mornings where she rolled over and was graced with that smile.

They stood there, two shadows beneath the soft glow of the streetlight, neither fully healed, but no longer tethered to a disappointing past. Kandice knew she had more to unpack, but when she leaned forward and Rebekah welcomed a soft kiss, she felt a little more weight fall away.

Chapter 10

REBEKAH

Rebekah sighed in relief as the last student exited the classroom with a wave. She didn't mind helping out with dismissal, but it was hard to keep her mind on things when all she could think about was having Kandice in her house in a few hours.

A week had passed, but Rebekah could still remember the exact moment the air between her and Kandice shifted. It was like gravity was pulling her back into something she had thought lost for good. After the movie night explosion and the emotionally raw conversation outside the bar, things between them had started to mend. Not all at once or with a grand sweeping declaration, but slowly and carefully. It was like the way someone might reassemble a broken vase—not trying to make it perfect again, but to find beauty in the cracks.

They had gone out to dinner two nights ago. Just a simple little Thai place in the next town over that had recently opened up. It was a cute place with low lights and music quiet enough to allow them to talk and get to know one another again. There were still nervous smiles reminiscent of first dates and new possibilities. In the end, when Rebekah had dropped Kandice back at her place, they had kissed again. It was quickly becoming Rebekah's new favorite pastime. The way Kandice's plush lips fit against hers had to be blasphemy. There was no way anything could have felt that right and not be fate. It hadn't answered every question, but it had made one thing certain: they weren't done. Not by a long shot.

It made tonight even more exciting and nerve-wracking. Tonight was their second *official* date. This time. They had chosen a more intimate location— Rebekah's house. No waiters. No public spaces. Just the two of them, homemade food and the endless weight of everything still unsaid.

Which explained why Rebekah had been staring at the clock on the wall for the last ten minutes like it held the secrets of the universe. A knock at the classroom door had her jerking in surprise. She rolled her eyes when she saw it was only Emma.

"You scared me," she said before standing up from her desk.

"Who did you think it was?" Emma asked as she stepped inside. "You pacing a hole into the tile yet?"

Rebekah groaned before dropping back down in her chair. "Maybe. Why? Did you come here to watch and laugh at my misery?"

"Maybe," Emma echoed before smiling. "Is it really wrong for me to want to see you panic in person?"

Rebekah rolled her eyes but let herself laugh. "I'm not panicking."

Emma raised an eyebrow. "Mmhmm. You're totally calm."

Rebekah groaned. "Okay, fine. Maybe I'm a *little* nervous."

"Because it's Kandice," Emma said, hopping up to sit on the edge of the desk. "And because it's not just a date. It's *history*. Emotionally loaded, high-stakes history."

"Helpful," Rebekah muttered. She picked at the top of her desk. "This isn't helping you know."

"I'm just saying," Emma said, more gently now. "It's okay to be nervous. You're trying again with someone who meant everything to you. That's not nothing."

Rebekah exhaled slowly before leaning back in her chair. "It's just…we were so close once. And then we weren't. And now I'm trying to balance between wanting things to feel like they used to and being terrified that they *will*—because last time, it ended in us not talking."

Emma tilted her head. "But it also started with friendship, right? That connection? The late nights talking about everything and nothing? The way you used to light up just talking about her?"

Rebekah gave her a side-eye. "You were *very* anti-Kandice for days after I told you what happened."

Emma shrugged. "It's because you're my bestie and I'd throw hands for you. But I've watched her lately. Or more specifically, I've watched her watch *you* and I'm liking what I see."

Before Rebekah could respond, a soft knock broke through their conversation and she looked over to see Kandice in the doorway.

"Rebekah?" Kandice's voice called gently.

Emma grinned. "Speak of the devil." She pitched her voice low, but Rebekah still gave her a look before turning her attention back to Kandice.

"Kandice. Hey. Everything okay?"

Kandice stepped into the classroom, smile slipping slightly when she looked between Rebekah and Emma. "Yeah, everything is good. Just wanted to check and make sure we're still on for tonight."

Rebekah smiled. "Yeah. Definitely."

There was a moment—one of those awkward pauses that stretched too long—before Kandice nodded, her shoulders relaxing. "Okay. I just didn't want to assume."

"No, feel free to assume away," Rebekah said, ignoring Emma's soft snicker.

Kandice's eyes flicked to Emma and back again. "Great. So…seven?"

"Sounds perfect," Rebekah said. Kandice smiled again, wider

this time and everything in Rebekah ached to reach out. Instead, she replied with a soft, "See you soon."

Kandice nodded before turning and leaving the way she came. As the door clicked shut behind her, Emma glanced over at Rebekah with a smirk. "Oh yeah. This date is going to go *very* well. I'm calling it."

Rebekah rolled her eyes, but her smile betrayed her. "Shut up."

"She smiled like a woman who likes you. That's all I'm saying."

Rebekah shook her head, but secretly she hoped Emma was right.

THE HOUSE SMELLED OF GARLIC, lemon, and roasted vegetables and yet Rebekah couldn't enjoy it. Her nerves had her damn near pacing in the kitchen as she put the final touches on everything. She had changed into something casual—jeans and a soft olive green top that Emma swore brought out her eyes. She'd pulled her hair back in a tight bun and even dabbed on a bit of easy makeup. She almost didn't recognize herself. It had been a long while since she had wanted to impress someone, and this wasn't just some random woman she met on a night out. Emma had been right about that. This was a big fucking deal.

With a sigh, she walked back over to the dining table and glared down at the cutlery. The table was set for two even though it could fit many more people around. She seldom used the dining table when it was just her. It was hard to eat there sometimes and not be reminded of her mother. They had spent some days just sitting quietly enjoying being together. It hadn't been the same without her even when Susan occasionally stayed over.

A knock at the front door pulled Rebekah from her melancholy thoughts, and she wiped her hands on her jeans before leaving the kitchen and heading for the front door. Each step forward had her heart pounding faster. When she opened the door to let Kandice in, the world paused for just a second.

Kandice looked beautiful.

Not in some dramatic, red-carpet type of way, but in a soft, lived-in way that felt like coming home after a long hard workday. She wore a denim jacket over a dark green sundress, with her hair pulled back loosely in soft waves, and she held a bottle of wine in one hand. Rebekah was nearly tongue-tied by how damn pretty she was.

"You look amazing," she breathed out before she could stop herself. Kandice's reaction was like a rose in bloom. Her smile was small, but wholly genuine, and she glanced down as if she were almost bashful at the attention. It took everything in Rebekah not to reach out and press that smile against her own lips.

"Thank you," Kandice said. Rebekah moved back to let her through the doorway and tried not to go weak at the knees by her enticing scent. "You look amazing as well."

Rebekah shrugged. "Yeah, well..." She trailed off not knowing what to say.

"Wow," Kandice said with a breathy smile as she stepped into the living room from the foyer. "Something smells amazing."

"Lemon chicken," Rebekah replied, taking the wine. "I was going to try something fancier, but I figured, why mess with a classic?"

Kandice smiled and followed her toward the kitchen. "You always did make amazing chicken."

They eased into conversation over dinner, the clink of silverware and the occasional shared laugh smoothing the tension that still hovered faintly between them. They talked about their students—Rebekah's class drama, Kandice's new lesson plan experiments, and about silly things like the staff room's horrible coffee. By the time they were clearing their plates and bringing them to the sink, something warm and electric had started pulsing under Rebekah's skin.

They stood at the sink together, sleeves rolled up, the soft hum of music playing from her Bluetooth speaker. Their shoulders bumped occasionally, and each time nearly had Rebekah jolting in place from the electricity that sparked between them. She could feel the quiet weight of Kandice's presence beside her. It was surprisingly not overwhelming and instead, grounding in a way. It was the kind of awareness that made her wonder if maybe they were supposed to be standing this close all along.

Kandice reached for a glass just as Rebekah turned to rinse another one, and their fingers brushed. They both froze. Rebekah glanced sideways and realized Kandice was already looking at her. How long had she been looking? Was Rebekah missing all the signs?

The music faded into the background as her thoughts took over. She opened her mouth, then closed it without saying a word. It almost felt like words would ruin this fragile anticipation between them.

Should I kiss her?

She wanted to. Badly. The moment was right there—ripe and ready to be plucked, but doubt crept in at the edges of her mind. What if she was misreading things? What if this was just comfort, not truly want? It was hard to get past the uncertainty of before even though she had said she wanted to try again to make something work between them.

Then Kandice leaned in just slightly. Just enough to close the space. "Can I kiss you?" Kandice asked, her voice barely above a whisper. Her eyes flitted down to Rebekah's lips. "I've wanted to kiss you all night."

Rebekah's heart stuttered. "Me too."

Kandice lifted her hand, water dripping off it. She reached up, gently cupping Rebekah's cheek. "You..." she started, her words catching.

Rebekah didn't wait for her to finish. Nothing about this kiss was tentative. It was soft, yes, but confident and familiar. It was a kiss that said, *we're doing this. We're here.* It had her dropping the glass she had been washing back into the sink not caring when the water splashed the front of her shirt. Kandice kissed her back immediately, stepping closer, her hand slipping to Rebekah's waist like it had always belonged there.

When they finally pulled back, Rebekah touched her forehead to Kandice's. They were both breathless—but smiling. It was almost a relief to have finally taken this step. Rebekah laughed, quiet and a little dazed.

"That was nice."

Kandice chuckled, brushing her thumb against Rebekah's cheek. "You always say 'nice' when you're flustered."

Rebekah groaned and buried her face in Kandice's shoulder. "Don't start calling me out already. We just got back on track."

Kandice wrapped both her arms around her, pulling her close. "Then let's stay on track."

They stood there for a while longer surrounded by the quiet rhythms of a home once filled with silence but now full of second chances partially realized. In that small, tender space between sink and candlelight, Rebekah finally let herself believe that this time, they might actually get it right.

Chapter 11

KANDICE

W as it possible to be addicted to kissing someone? That had to be why Kandice found it impossible to stop kissing Rebekah. They had stood at the kitchen sink for what felt like hours trading soft kisses back and forth until Kandice's lips buzzed with electricity, and she felt the need to lie down, preferably with Rebekah's warmth in her arms.

"I could kiss you forever," Rebekah whispered. Those words nearly demolished all of Kandice's thoughts about taking things slowly. She wanted this with the type of desire that nearly upended her, but she was still terrified of getting things wrong. She was just lucky that Rebekah hadn't written her off for good, apology or not.

"I was thinking the same thing," she admitted softly before dipping in for another hit from Rebekah's lips. As far as kisses went, Kandice had had plenty, but none so consuming. It was as if every nerve in her body was connected to where the skin of Rebekah's lips met hers, and she brought her hands up to clutch at Rebekah's blouse. They fit together like perfect puzzle pieces and when Rebekah's tongue asked for entrance between Kandice's lips, she parted them eagerly groaning at the hint of citrus and

Rebekah's own unique flavor. Rebekah's soft moan laid siege to the last tendrils of Kandice's control as her body clenched with the need for *more*. It was that thought, that deep desire for more that gave Kandice the strength to pull back.

"Maybe we should take this somewhere less...watery." Her voice had gone husky with want but she didn't have it in her to care. Not when Rebekah's eyes were half-lidded and filled with the same desire that was no doubt reflected in her own gaze.

Rebekah's lips twitched. "Less watery, huh? Not sure if that's possible."

Kandice rolled her eyes. "You know what I mean." This teasing was new for her. Her sex life with Charles hadn't been quite as fun or carefree. Even from the beginning it was almost clinical. She hadn't known that it should be any different. But now, with Rebekah cracking jokes even as they kissed their way up the stairs, she could easily see that she had missed out on a lot over the years. She had so much to make up for. Before she could second guess herself, she grabbed Rebekah's hand and pulled it down to press against her lower stomach.

"If you're done teasing me about my words, you can see the type of wetness I was hoping we could focus on." The words were bold for her and Kandice's cheeks burned at her own daring. She couldn't regret anything when she saw Rebekah's eyes widen before going molten.

"Who taught you how to be so dirty?" She asked as she moved her hand shaking off Kandice's. "You better know what you're asking me, because we never had dessert and I'm still more than a little hungry."

Kandice swallowed hard, mouth gone dry at not only Rebekah's words but also her tone. There was promise there—the type of promise that she knew would rearrange her entire being. Her cunt pulsed with the need for it. Before she could feel embarrassment for how turned on she was, she pushed Rebekah away.

"Oh?" She asked breathlessly as she raised her hands to the

straps of her dress. She was glad she had left her jacket downstairs because it made it easy for her to lift the fabric from her shoulders and let it fall around her. Kandice stood there, refusing to let her nerves get the best of her. "You're awfully dressed for someone who—"

Her voice cut off with a soft wheeze when Rebekah reached out trailing fingers against her neck. That wicked touch lit up her nerves as it trailed between the valley of her breasts and over the trembling skin of her stomach.

"Get on the bed."

That voice rang out with authority, making Kandice shiver. She had never heard Rebekah sound like that, but damnit if she didn't want to hear it more. The woman in front of her had shifted somehow becoming something new and yet achingly familiar.

"You think you can just order me around and I'll go willingly?" Kandice asked, unable to stop her last bit of defiance. She had to lock her knees as she watched Rebekah walk closer to her, hips swaying slowly. Her warmth bled into her even through the fabric of Rebekah's clothes. Kandice swallowed hard again when Rebekah gripped her chin softly.

They were the same height, and yet somehow Rebekah seemed to loom over her. Dark brown eyes watched her silently before Rebekah finally spoke again.

"Yes." The word was almost purred, and Kandice's nerves were alight as the sound of it washed over her. "I think you will get on the bed willingly. I think you will willingly spread those gorgeous thighs so I can get between them and show you all the ways you can have pleasure that I *know* that ex of yours never bothered to. And when you come, I think it will be my name you willingly drop from your lips."

"Fuck," Kandice bit out before Rebekah pulled her in. She wanted to rant and curse and fight back, but all she could do was melt into the embrace, hands gripping the front of Rebekah's shirt as if it were the only thing keeping her from falling. Warm fingers gripped her chin tightly as her lips were expertly pried open. The groan that slipped out when a tongue darted forward dueling with her own was damning and rocked her to her very core. How was she supposed to resist this? Her body yearned to touch and be touched, to taste and be tasted, and she wanted to give in. Her hands tangled in cloth, unsure whether to push back or pull forward, as her breathing sped up.

The hand at her chin loosened, sliding along her cheek until it was buried in the hair at the base of her neck. The sure grip seemed at odds with the soft curves pressed against her chest, but it was a thrilling difference. She reached up to wrap her arms around Rebekah's shoulders and the back of her hands accidentally brushed across hard straining nipples. Kandice felt her blood ignite at the soft moan that drifted from Rebekah's lips. It seemed she wasn't the only one affected by their kisses; kisses that seemed to grow wetter and needier with each second that slid by. When she felt soft sheets against her back, her desperation to feel Rebekah's warm weight pressing her down as they ate from each other ravenously grew. The wet sounds of their kiss made Kandice's skin prickle and all she could think about was *more.*

Rebekah kept herself propped up and Kandice grunted in annoyance. Rebekah's chuckle was dark as she moved separating their mouths.

"Don't pout," Rebekah said with a smile. "I'm just moving to get my clothes off too."

"Well, hurry," Kandice panted out, forcing herself not to reach up and pull her back down. She waited impatiently, enjoying each bit of skin as it was revealed to her. When Rebekah reached for her own bra, Kandice arched her back and did the same. Once it was unclasped, she tossed it and her panties, not caring where they went. She just wanted to feel Rebekah's bare skin against hers as quickly as possible.

Rebekah's skin was deep like warm earth and almost glowed with its own inner heat. She smelled of coconut and rich honey making Kandice's mouth water with the need to savor. This hunger was a new one but one she needed to satiate as soon as possible. When her eyes fell on the dark brush of hair that covered Rebekah's pussy, Kandice's hunger surged.

"Here," she said, tapping on Rebekah's thighs. "Move up here. Closer. I want to see you."

"Fuck," Rebekah groaned.

"That's the idea." Kandice giggled when Rebekah thumped her forehead. She reached out, guiding Rebekah to perch above her chest. "God, come closer so I can taste you."

"You—" Rebekah's voice was choked to a stop when Kandice lifted her head. She breathed deeply, exhaling from her mouth. "Fuck. If you're sure."

"I am." There was no hesitance in Kandice's voice. There was a small bit of anxiety in her mind, namely for if she would be good at this, but that was it. She didn't hesitate to pull Rebekah again, sighing softly when she finally settled more fully on her face. With the first lick of her tongue, Kandice was gone.

Rebekah tasted of musk and something more undeniably her. She was blood hot and engorged against Kandice's lips. Kandice dug her nails into the skin of Rebekah's thigh as she sipped, letting her tongue press deep into Rebekah's hole. Loud slurps had her cheeks hot but it only fueled her to go faster and push deeper.

Rebekah's hands settled on top of her head holding her in place. She could feel more trembles shooting through Rebekah's body and her own pussy pulsed with answering need. Kandice didn't see any reason to deny herself. She let go of one of Rebekah's thighs and reached down to press a finger against her own slick lips. Her eyes were only half open as she looked up at Rebekah.

"Fuck, look at you," Rebekah whispered as she traced a finger over Kandice's cheek. Her voice was husky and the sound of it made Kandice groan. "You love this don't you? Eating me out— having me ride your face."

Kandice nodded as much as she could. When Rebekah looked over her shoulder, a whine left her. She knew Rebekah could see her plunging two of her own fingers deep in her cunt. Kandice couldn't believe how turned on she was.

"Are you wet just from having your tongue in my pussy?"

God. Was it possible to pass out from arousal? Kandice wasn't sure, but if it was, she was probably close. She shifted her head up, flicking her tongue over Rebekah's clit and enjoying the way she jolted on top of her. The hand on top of her head suddenly gripped tightly and Kandice had to close her eyes against the pulse of pure want that shot through her at the rougher treatment. She was discovering so many new things about herself tonight.

"I'm going to come," Rebekah panted out as she shifted her hips, riding Kandice's face harder. Slick sounds danced around Kandice's ears, and she sucked in a sharp breath when her tongue breached Rebekah's hole again. She wanted to glut herself on that slick liquid until it flavored her breath. She didn't hesitate to shift her arm until she could rub her thumb over Rebekah's clit.

A feedback loop of pleasure coursed through her as she strained upward. Kandice's pussy was damn near drenched leaving her inner thighs slick as she plunged her fingers deep. Rebekah's grip on her hair never loosened, keeping Kandice's face firmly against her cunt as she spasmed.

"Kandice."

The sound of her name falling from Rebekah's lips had her locking up and Kandice moaned loudly when she came, her own thumb pressing hard against her engorged nub. It wasn't until her orgasm waned that she realized Rebekah was leaned over her, chest rising and falling rapidly with each breath. When she saw Kandice looking at her, she didn't straighten, but she did lift her hips up enough to move away. Rebekah rolled over on her back.

"Are you okay?"

Kandice thought about it as she pulled her fingers from her pussy. Was she okay? She was a little sore and still fairly stuffed from dinner, but beyond that, she felt amazing. Better than she had in a long while and she made sure to tell Rebekah that.

"I feel great."

Rebekah glanced over with a smile that slowly turned wicked. Before Kandice could ask what was up, Rebekah had rolled back over on top of her. "Don't think that we're done now," Rebekah said with a grin. She pressed a teasing kiss to Kandice's lips. "Is your mom okay watching Caleb for the night?"

Kandice nodded. "Yeah, of course. Why?"

Rebekah brushed her fingers across Kandice's bare neck. "Because I'm not letting you out of this bed until dawn."

Chapter 12

REBEKAH

Waking up with Kandice warm and heavy in her arms was on Rebekah's list of top ways to wake up. Last night had been more than everything she had hoped for. Dinner had gone well enough, but what happened after—Kandice pulling her down and attacking her pussy like she had been half-starved for days was nothing short of magical. She was still mind blown that Kandice had never eaten pussy before.

Now, with Kandice warm in her arms, Rebekah couldn't help but be glad that Charles and Riley were shit people. She wasn't happy that Kandice had to go through a betrayal like that, but it had been what led them to reconnect something she hadn't truly believed possible. With a sigh, she rolled over onto her side wrapping her arms around Kandice fully and burying her face in her neck. They had showered before falling into bed together and Kandice smelled so much like her that it tugged at a hunger in Rebekah. Normally, she was slow to wake but right now everything was firing on all cylinders. She knew Kandice needed to get home later this morning. She was a mom and one thing Rebekah wouldn't do was encroach on Kandice's time with her son. But that meant if she wanted to fit more alone time in, she would need to make a move.

Rebekah stretched before pressing soft kisses against Kandice's neck. She looked up when Kandice shifted and smiled when she scrunched her nose up.

"You are adorable," she whispered before kissing slowly over Kandice's cheek. "So fucking adorable I could just eat you right up."

Kandice hummed softly. "Didn't you get enough of me last night?" Her voice was rough from sleep and Rebekah thought it sounded heavenly.

"Never," she whispered fiercely before drawing back to look at her. Kandice's eyes were half-open, and her lips were curved up in a fond smile. The way she looked lying there in Rebekah's bed was almost too much to handle. "I don't think I'll ever get enough of you," Rebekah said, eyes locked on Kandice's lips.

Kandice giggled softly before bringing a hand up to cup Rebekah's cheek. "You are wonderful."

"Flattery will get you fucked." That wasn't exactly what she meant to say, but Rebekah found she didn't want to take it back. Something about this—waking up with the woman she had truthfully always wanted beside her was revving her up in the best way. "It's my turn to take you apart."

When Kandice didn't protest, Rebekah surged forward, their lips coming together so hard their teeth nearly knocked together. She swallowed Kandice's chuckle and pushed her tongue forward until it swept the roof of the other woman's mouth. She could taste the faint bite of morning on Kandice's tongue as it moved against hers desperately like she wanted that as much as Rebekah. Hands gripped and pulled until they were once again pressed together as tight as they could be, bare skin brushing and catching creating heat under the blanket. Rebekah could feel her skin starting to sweat but she didn't care. All she cared about was getting closer and pressing harder. She wanted bruises so she could press on them later and remember exactly how it felt to be with Kandice.

Kandice pulled away to gulp in much needed air. Rebekah, not wanting to waste any time, took that as an invitation to taste the sweet skin of her neck. She enjoyed the breathy moan that vibrated from Kandice's throat and reached up to grip Kandice's hair to angle the other woman's head back further. Rebekah felt powerful and confident as Kandice surrendered to her need to taste every part of her. It was a thrilling feeling to have someone she wanted for so long practically begging for her touch. Rebekah knew then that she would never be able to get enough. She was spoiled for anyone else.

"Rebekah..." Kandice trailed off. Her voice was rough with passion and her hands ran up and down Rebekah's back as if unsure where to touch next.

Rebekah arched into the feeling even as she attacked the other side of Kandice's neck with vigor. Her teeth lightly nipped at Kandice's pulse point, enjoying the way it fluttered against her tongue in a quick staccato beat. One of Rebekah's hands unwound itself from Kandice's hair and slid down until her fingers could dance across Kandice's collar bone.

Kandice sighed and rolled fully on her back and Rebekah followed, lips never leaving her prize. She stared down in awe at the woman before her. Kandice's head was thrown back in pleasure. Her eyes were tightly closed, and her kiss bitten lips were parted slightly letting puffs of air sail through.

"Gorgeous," Rebekah whispered.

Kandice's eyes opened and when their eyes met, Rebekah could have sworn that she felt a physical charge pass between them. She shivered as another wave of arousal crashed through her body.

"You have no idea how long I've waited for this," Rebekah whispered heatedly. She leaned her head down until she could brush her lips against Kandice's own. "I always knew you would be like this; hungry and so fucking sweet." Rebekah brought her hand around and brushed Kandice's bottom lip with her thumb.

Kandice looked at her for a moment before cupping her cheek and bringing their faces together. She brushed her lips against Rebekah's, the kiss so sweet it had Rebekah's heart thumping harshly. This type of intimacy Rebekah had never experienced before, and she didn't think she ever would again. It made her want to hold on tight and never let go.

Rebekah's gaze slowly slid down Kandice's frame taking in the fluttering of the pulse at her neck, the light sheen of sweat already gathering on her skin and Kandice's glorious breasts and dark brown nipples.

"Fuck," Rebekah whispered as her mouth watered with the need to taste, a need she had no desire to fight. The first touch of her tongue against Kandice's nipple had them both moaning in pleasure. She went down on her elbows as she lavished that delicious peak with eager licks and kisses. Her other hand wasn't idle, paying heed to the other nipple, pinching lightly and then a bit harder when Kandice moaned. Nails dug into her back spurring her on.

"You taste so fucking good," Rebekah gasped out before switching to the other nipple. She loved how it peaked in her mouth, tightening into a little bud. She pressed Kandice down, settling her torso between Kandice's legs. The heat between them flared as soft grunts and whimpers filled the air. "God, I love hearing you like this."

Hands gripped the back of her head coaxing her back up. Mouths, fevered and relentless, met over and over as they ravenously fed from one another. Kandice moved until one of her legs pressed between Rebekah's. The pressure had Rebekah gasping and Kandice smirked. She pushed her thigh tighter moving it up and down. Rebekah, refusing to be outmaneuvered, gripped that devious thigh and shifted until she was once again between Kandice's spread legs.

"You think you're clever."

Kandice shrugged before smirking. "Maybe. Or maybe, I just know your weaknesses."

Rebekah chuckled darkly. "Don't underestimate me." She slid her hand up the sensitive inner skin of Kandice's thigh until the tips of her fingers brushed against neatly trimmed hair. The hitch in Kandice's breath drove Rebekah wild and she dipped forward gathering some of Kandice's slick before bringing her fingers to her own lips. She licked her fingers once and then again enjoying the burn of Kandice's gaze.

"You are a menace," Kandice groaned out.

"Are you really surprised by that?"

Kandice paused before shaking her head. "Not even a little bit."

"Good." Rebekah dropped down kissing Kandice deeply again. She swallowed down the whining moan that Kandice let out when Rebekah pressed a finger between her pussy lips. The easy slide inside had Rebekah almost wishing she had a dick. She could only imagine how good that would feel when it felt this damn good with a finger.

"So good," Kandice panted out. She shifted her grip, fingers digging into the back of Rebekah's neck. "Give me another."

Rebekah chuckled. "So bossy." Still, she didn't deny her, pulling out her finger before sliding it and another back inside. Kandice's pussy was perfect and warm, its slick walls shifting against her skin. She moved back and down wanting to see. "Look at how good you take my fingers."

"I would say take a picture, but I don't want anything getting out."

"I wouldn't anyway," Rebekah agreed. "This is only for my eyes and my memory." She leaned forward, shaking off Kandice's hold. She'd tasted her last night as they explored one another, but the second hit was just as good as the first. The slick sounds of her fingers plunging in and out had her cheeks heating and her tongue joined, winding between her fingers.

Kandice's moans filled the air, and she threw off the blanket making Rebekah shiver. The cooler air didn't stop her as she curled her fingers up, pressing with each pass. She brushed her nose against Kandice's clit before wrapping her lips around it and sucking. The effect was instantaneous. Kandice's thighs closed around her as a hand shot down again gripping the back of her neck.

"Don't stop," Kandice begged as her hips began to move. Rebekah had no intention to. She sped up her movements riding the dips and flows of Kandice's hips as she moved into the feeling. Kandice's thighs began to tremble, and Rebekah's stomach growled wanting more of that taste. She continued to lavish that clit with flicks of her tongue. She could feel Kandice growing close and she wanted to hear her voice ring out as she came.

"Plea—" Kandice's voice cut off as her hips jerked, nearly slamming into Rebekah's nose. Rebekah didn't let up, continuing to curl her fingers as wetness covered her fingers and chin. Her stomach clenched when she realized Kandice had squirted, just a little, with the force of her orgasm. Kandice's body continued to tremble as Rebekah thrust her fingers wanting to draw out her pleasure. Eventually, it seemed her strings were cut, sending Kandice crashing back onto the bed as her thighs continued to jerk.

"Fuck," she groaned tossing her head to the side. When she pushed Rebekah's face away, Rebekah went reluctantly. She enjoyed the way Kandice's legs shook and the slick sound of her fingers sliding from that perfect hole.

"Damn that was hot," Rebekah growled out before sucking her fingers into her mouth. Kandice threw an arm over her face.

"That has never happened before."

Rebekah chuckled as she leaned over Kandice. She moved her arm out of the way. "Get used to it. Now that I know it's possible, I will be actively trying to make it happen again."

"Your bed will never survive."

"I have a waterproof mattress protector," Rebekah pointed out with a shark-like grin. "I'll get new sheets and a few more towels. We'll be fine."

Kandice gave her a level look. "It sounds like you're planning things out."

Rebekah swallowed hard before jumping all in. "I am. If that's okay with you." She brushed her clean fingers over Kandice's cheek. "I spent years not thinking I would ever get to talk to you again. Now that this is happening, I'll fight like hell to make it work."

Kandice stared at her a moment before her lips split in a wide smile. "Me too." She tilted her head up and Rebekah answered the plea brushing their lips together in a soft kiss. "But for now, I think we need to shower and get some actual food."

"We could shower together," Rebekah suggested.

Kandice snorted. "That worked so well last night. No, I'll shower down the hall so we can actually make it downstairs and have breakfast before I head home." At Rebekah's pout, she leaned forward and pressed their foreheads together. "Don't worry. I want to have this as much as I can too."

Rebekah nodded feeling better than she had in a long while. "That's good enough for me."

Chapter 13

KANDICE

K andice had barely stepped into the kitchen when furious knocking at the front door made her pause. She and Rebekah had showered separately, and she was the first one down. She could hear Rebekah's footsteps upstairs, but she wasn't sure if Rebekah had heard the knocking. She was torn. This wasn't her house, so she didn't think it would be right if she answered the door.

"Rebekah," she called out, glancing at the foyer. "Beks. There's someone at the front door."

The furious knocking started again this time followed by thumping steps on the stairs.

"Kandice?" Rebekah asked when she got to the bottom step. "What's going on? I thought I heard—" The knocking interrupted her.

"Were you expecting someone this morning?" Kandice asked.

Rebekah shook her head. "No. I wonder who the hell it is. Emma would have called before coming over today." Kandice waited at the kitchen doorway while Rebekah went over and opened the front door.

"Susan? What the hell are you doing here?" Rebekah's voice sounded shocked and a fair bit annoyed.

Kandice's stomach dropped. She vaguely recognized that name as Rebekah's ex-girlfriend. With the door open, light filtered in illuminating her. That only lasted until she pushed past Rebekah into the house. She stopped when she saw Kandice standing in the kitchen doorway.

Susan glared; light-blue eyes filled with clear disdain. Her dark brown hair was pulled up in a messy bun and her lightly tanned cheeks were stained with color. Kandice realized how it looked given she was only clothed in a pair of shorts and a t-shirt, both borrowed from Rebekah.

"What am I doing here? What the fuck is she doing here?" Her voice went shrill as she pointed at Kandice. Kandice raised her eyebrows but didn't say anything. She was comforted when Rebekah crossed her arms leaving the front door wide open.

"She was invited, Susan. You were not." She gestured to the door. "What is the issue? Why are you knocking on my door so early in the morning?"

Kandice ignored the part of her that wanted to say anything. This wasn't her house, and it wasn't her show. Plus, an eager part of her wanted to hear what Rebekah had to say in the face of her ex's ire.

Susan swayed a little in front of them. "I came because you mean a lot to me, and I wanted to talk to you and then I see her here." Susan continued pointing a finger at Kandice angrily. "The same person who's been messing with your head the whole fucking time just because she can't decide if she likes dick or not."

Kandice had to grit her teeth to keep from saying something she might later regret. Her sexuality was only relevant for Rebekah, and while she wasn't sure if she would ever be attracted to another man, she knew that what she felt for Rebekah was stronger than anything else she had felt in her nearly thirty years of life. This wasn't just friendship. Friends didn't find heaven buried tongue deep in their friend's pussy. These feelings were anything but platonic.

"We've only been broken up for a month and already you're letting some random bitch move into my spot without even talking to me," Susan continued. She turned to Rebekah, hands on her hips. "You didn't even talk to me about this."

"Let's get something straight," Rebekah said, her voice falling into a deeper timber that had Kandice standing up straighter and taking notice. She had briefly heard threads of that tone last night and she found it just as intriguing now as she had then. "You broke up with me to go move in with someone you knew for two weeks."

"I was just confused," Susan explained as she walked over to Rebekah. "You were always talking about the future here in this town, but I know if we went back to Cali, you could start again and really make it this time."

Kandice froze. Rebekah had never mentioned wanting to move back west. From all the signs she'd seen, Rebekah had seemed happy working with her students and inspiring some of them to continue music into high school and beyond. Nothing about their conversations had pointed towards Rebekah wanting to try again at making it big in the music industry.

"This town is too small for your talent," Susan continued. She put a hand on Rebekah's arm as she looked up at her. As Kandice looked on, it hurt to see how well Susan and Rebekah could have fit together.

Susan had that video girl figure, with full hips and a trim waist. She was a couple inches shorter than Rebekah and even Kandice. She would probably fit under the curve of Rebekah's arm better than Kandice. Insecurity crept into her thoughts the longer Susan talked.

"And you always said you didn't want kids."

"No," Rebekah said, her voice ringing out in the hallway. She pushed Susan away gently. "I always said I didn't want kids with you. And I'm not moving back to L.A. because I don't want to. I don't feel trapped here."

Susan stumbled back, her fists clenched at her sides. "Oh please. You can't be serious about staying in this podunk ass town."

"I am serious."

"Why? Because of her?" Susan said, her voice rising as she pointed at Kandice again. She glared over at her. "She isn't even divorced from her cheating ass ex-husband, and you really want to throw away everything we had for her?"

Now, Kandice did speak up. Clearly, people in town had been running their mouths about her situation, but she was done being ashamed. Her past was her past, but she was moving forward. "My ongoing divorce is none of your business, Susan. Regardless, what happens is between Rebekah and me. She knows me and she knows my heart."

"Oh please," Susan spit out. "This won't last."

"I think it's time you left," Rebekah said, her voice quiet but firm. When Susan tried to protest, Rebekah sighed and rubbed a hand over her face. "Look, Susan. You knew going into this that I had feelings for Kandice. Our relationship was always on and off because both you and I knew it wasn't going to last. It's why I didn't protest when you moved on. We always knew it had an expiration date."

Rebekah walked past Susan and stood back next to Kandice. She took Kandice's hand and smiled. Kandice squeezed her hand, lending her strength. When she glanced back over at Susan, she almost felt bad for her. If they weren't both vying for the same woman, that is.

"I know how it hurts to not be wanted by someone you love," Kandice said gently. "But I'm with Rebekah because I have real feelings for her. You might not understand, and you might not agree, but that's the truth."

"Fuck you!" Kandice flinched at Susan's shout. Susan's eyes

were watery with unshed tears and her thin lips were pressed into a harsh line as she glanced back and forth at them. "Fuck you both." For a moment, Kandice thought the other woman might break down. Instead, she turned and stomped down the porch stairs.

"Well, that is one way to wake up in the morning," Rebekah said with a sigh. Kandice's gaze was still focused on Susan's retreating back, but she let her body go soft and pliant as Rebekah wrapped an arm around her shoulders. "Sorry about that."

Kandice shook her head and wrapped an arm around Rebekah's waist leaning into her. "It's not your fault. Hell, I have an entire ex-husband who has disliked you since we were in high school. It's only right that I deal with a disgruntled ex-girlfriend or two."

Rebekah laughed and pressed a kiss to Kandice's cheek. "Only one. I was too busy taking care of mom to really date and Susan was the only one who didn't take things too seriously." She paused. "At least, I thought she didn't."

"It's fine," Kandice insisted. She pushed Rebekah to the door. "You go close that and I'll raid your refrigerator to see what we can scrounge up for breakfast." She giggled when Rebekah turned pulling her back again.

"Or we could throw on some clothes, swing by to get Caleb and Margie and all go to brunch."

Kandice's chest warmed. "Are you sure? I don't want to rush you into anything."

Rebekah shook her head. "I'm the one who asked. And frankly, in my opinion we've been edging each other to death for the past decade. If anything, we've probably taken things too slow." She leaned forward brushing her lips against Kandice's. "I know you still have a lot to figure out and get through, but I want you to know I'm all in. I've been in love with you since I knew what love was. You're kind of it for me."

Kandice's stomach clenched and yet, she wasn't scared. Those words should have terrified her after the way her marriage imploded, but all she could feel was relief. Kandice's eyes burned at Rebekah's soft admission. She couldn't say it back, not yet. She didn't want to lie to anyone anymore and that meant being truthful even when it hurt. Instead, she placed a soft kiss on Rebekah's lips and rubbed their noses together.

The action seemed to speak for itself. Rebekah pulled her closer until Kandice's head rested against her neck. Kandice wrapped her arms around Rebekah's waist snuggling as close as she could with a content sigh.

Everything would be okay. She would make sure of that.

Epilogue

KANDICE

ONE YEAR LATER...

K andice hadn't expected the courthouse to be so quiet.

The finalization of her divorce from Charles took all of twenty minutes—twenty clinical, almost mechanical minutes of signatures, legal jargon, and the strange weightlessness of something once so heavy being officially over. She'd half-expected a wave of grief, maybe even regret, to engulf her. Especially when Charles hadn't once asked about Caleb. Instead, what settled over her was peace. Well, that and something new. Something light. It was like she had been holding her breath for the past ten years and could finally exhale.

Outside the courthouse, the San Diego sun spilled across the pavement in that golden, west coast way—soft and glimmering. The palm trees swayed in the salty breeze. It was a far cry from landlocked Georgia. She had thought coming back would make her miss California, but she found it just the opposite. Everything was too loud and too much. She longed to go back to Hickory Springs where the days stretched out quieter and less hurried. Beside her, Rebekah smiled, her fingers brushing against Kandice's as they walked toward the parked rental car.

"Well," Rebekah said, her tone light but laced with something quiet and meaningful. "You're officially a single woman."

Kandice smirked, giving her a playful sideways glance. "Am I, though?"

Rebekah lifted a brow. "You did just sign papers ending a marriage."

"True. But my heart's already been stolen," Kandice replied, bumping their shoulders together gently. "So technically, I'm still taken, just by someone else."

Rebekah's laugh was low and warm, the kind of laugh that always made Kandice feel like she was home. "Guess we'll have to celebrate that too."

Kandice stopped walking and tugged gently on Rebekah's hand to make her stop too. "We could go back to the hotel," she said, tilting her head slightly, letting her grin turn just a little wicked. "Finish celebrating. Properly."

"Oh?" Rebekah's eyes sparkled with amusement. "Are you suggesting something indecent, Ms. Newly Single?"

"Absolutely," Kandice said, already leading the way to the car. "You're corrupting me."

"I think you were halfway corrupted before I got here."

They both laughed, and Kandice felt the tightness in her chest begin to loosen entirely.

The ride back to the hotel was quiet, but not in a tense way. More like the quiet after a long storm, when all the thunder had passed and the only thing left was the soft patter of rain and the distant, echoing peace of something that no longer had power over you. Rebekah reached over at a stoplight and rested her hand on Kandice's knee. It wasn't even a big gesture, just casual, familiar, and grounding—but Kandice felt it go all the way through her.

They pulled into the hotel parking garage and rode the elevator up in silence. The hotel was nice, but it wasn't five-star material.

The carpet was that same forgettable beige every hotel seemed to have, and the overhead lights were a little too bright. But none of it mattered—not with Rebekah's fingers brushing hers and definitely not with the way her heart beat a little faster now that it was just the two of them again.

Their room was tucked at the end of the hall, away from the elevators and away from the noise. Kandice fished the keycard out of her purse and slipped it into the lock. It blinked green, and she opened the door, stepping into the cool, dim room that already smelled faintly of Rebekah's vanilla body lotion and the room service coffee they hadn't finished that morning. Rebekah followed her in, setting her purse down gently on the table by the window. Kandice didn't turn on the lights. She liked it this way. It reminded her of quiet mornings when she stayed over at Rebekah's. They always woke together, enjoying a quiet moment of coffee in bed as they simply sat together enjoying each other's company.

Kandice turned to face Rebekah, her heart pounding a little now. Not from nerves but from something bigger. From the thoughts she'd been carrying for weeks, maybe even longer.

Rebekah was looking at her like she already knew something was amiss. "Are you okay?"

Kandice nodded quickly. "Yeah, I'm fine. I just...have something I wanted to tell you."

"Alright," Rebekah replied as she pulled Kandice over to the bed. She sat on the edge of it parting her legs so Kandice could stand between. "What's up?"

"I love you," Kandice blurted out without fanfare. She hadn't planned to say it like that. She'd been rehearsing the words in her down time when Rebekah wasn't around. Margie had even walked in on her saying it once or twice and simply walked out with a knowing smirk on her face. Kandice hadn't thought about how it would sound out loud, but in this moment, it came out steady and true. She had no hesitation about it. She knew she loved Rebekah.

Rebekah blinked once. "Yeah?" she asked softly, eyes shining. "You mean it?"

"I do." Kandice nodded, and her voice didn't shake. "I love you, Rebekah. I think I started to fall for you the second I moved back home. Hell, maybe even before that. Maybe the reason Charles was such an ass is because he knew it was you my heart really wanted."

It was something that she had been contemplating for a while. The thought that Charles had possibly realized the depth of Kandice's feelings for Rebekah and sought to remove her before Kandice realized. She doubted she would ever really find out the truth of that, but she was content in the knowledge that she was free to do as she pleased now.

"Being with you has always felt easy. You and me just felt right. And now? Now it feels real. Like I finally let go of everything that wasn't meant for me."

Rebekah let out a shaky breath before pulling Kandice closer. She reached up and gently took Kandice's face in her hands.

"I love you, too," she said, voice barely above a whisper.

Kandice laughed quietly, her forehead resting against Rebekah's. "I had been planning how to say it to you for months, and then here I go just blurting it out in a hotel room. So much for romance and the right moment."

"If you ask me, this was a pretty perfect moment." When Kandice frowned, she explained, "It's you and me together. That is always going to equal perfection."

There was nothing Kandice could say in that moment. Words failed her, but she knew kisses never would. She pressed her lips against Rebekah's—not rushed or frantic, but slow and thorough. This kiss was intentional. It was the kind of kiss that said, *I see you. I choose you. For life.*

Kandice wrapped her arms around Rebekah's shoulders and pulled her close. Everything else, the courthouse, the flight home tomorrow, even the conversations she knew she would still have to have with Caleb, melted away. All that remained was this. Rebekah's warmth and her steady hands. Her lips pressed gently against Kandice's, like they had all the time in the world.

Later, as they laid side by side on the hotel bed, Kandice marveled at how life had a way of circling back. The city buzzed outside their room, but inside, everything was soft and intimate. She stared at the ceiling, fingers loosely laced with Rebekah's.

"Is it weird that I don't feel sad at all?"

"No," Rebekah said, her voice calm and low. "You already did the grieving a long time ago."

"I think you're right." Kandice glanced over at her. "Don't get used to me saying that."

Rebekah laughed, squeezing her hand. "That man never deserved you."

"Well," Kandice murmured, "he definitely doesn't now."

The sun slowly dipped below the horizon washing the room in burnt orange and purples. They continued to lay there, skin warm against skin, fingers gently exploring familiar territory. The continued quiet between them was full of meaning, full of all the words that didn't need to be said because they were already known. Kandice rolled onto her side to look at Rebekah.

"You know, I didn't think I'd get to have this," she said. "Not after everything. I thought I'd be one of those people who stayed broken. Or settled. Or just quietly lonely."

"You're not broken," Rebekah said, tracing her fingers slowly along Kandice's forearm. "You never were. You just weren't where you were supposed to be yet."

Kandice swallowed past the sudden lump in her throat. "You sound so sure."

"I am," Rebekah said firmly, her eyes soft. "You came back to town like this storm I wasn't expecting. I didn't know how much I missed you until I saw you again. And I definitely didn't know how much I could still love someone until you made space for me to."

"This thing between us…it's not a rebound, Rebekah. It's not just comfort. It's real. And it's good."

Rebekah exhaled. "Good. We'll take it all day by day. Together."

Kandice nodded, feeling the calm settle deep in her bones. "Together sounds pretty damn good."

They fell asleep that way—entwined and content, no longer haunted by the past or afraid of the future. For the first time in years, Kandice felt like she was right where she belonged.

About Karmen Lee

Karmen Lee is an author of diverse and queer adult contemporary and steamy romance. She's a single mom living it up in Atlanta, Georgia with her kid, her cats, and humidity. When she's not carpooling or packing lunches, you can probably find her enjoying a glass of wine and dreaming up ways to show her readers a good time.

Also by Karmen Lee

Dummond Siblings

Passion Over Pride

Passion Over Power

Coffee Shops of Love

Cups of You

Sips of Her

Tastes of Him

Standalone Novellas

Finding Forever With You: A Second-Chance Novella

Only For The Night: A Sweet Temptations Novella

Her Christmas Wish: A Sweet Heat Holiday Novella

Sipping & Swooning: A Sweet Heat Holiday Novella

Changing Spaces: A Clover Hill Romance

From Afterglow Books

The 7-10 Split: A Romantic Comedy

The Relationship Mechanic

The Secret Crush Book Club (Out August 2025)